Porter Wyman.

She didn't want to think about *him*. She didn't want to think about *any* man, not in a personal way. Generic thoughts about him and his baby were harmless. But dwelling on the man himself was not a good idea.

What was there about the rancher turned businessman that had snagged her attention in the first place? Admittedly, he was good-looking in a rugged sort of way, with his dark hair, chocolate eyes and athletic build. But attractive or not, a slow-grinning man who had an infant to raise wasn't for her.

For so long she hadn't given any man the time of day, much less anything else. And she wasn't going to give *Porter* anything else, either.

Dear Reader,

Hectic life? Too much to do, too little time? Well, Silhouette Desire provides you with the perfect emotional getaway with this month's moving stories of men and women finding love and passion. So relax, pick up a Desire novel and let yourself escape, with six wonderful, involving, totally absorbing romances.

Ultratalented author Mary Lynn Baxter kicks off November with her sultry Western style in *Slow Talkin' Texan*, the story of a MAN OF THE MONTH whose strong desires collide with an independent lady—she's silk to his denim, lace to his leather... and doing all she can to resist this *irresistible* tycoon. A small-town lawman who rescues a "lost" beauty might just find his own Christmas bride in Jennifer Greene's heartwarming *Her Holiday Secret*. Ladies, watch closely as a *Thirty-Day Fiancé* is transformed into a forever husband in Leanne Banks's third book in THE RULEBREAKERS miniseries.

Don't dare miss the intensity of an innocent wife trying to seduce her honor-bound husband in *The Oldest Living Married Virgin*, the latest in Maureen Child's spectacular miniseries THE BACHELOR BATTALION. And when a gorgeous ex-marine shows up at his old flame's ranch to round up the "wife who got away," he discovers a daughter he never knew in *The Re-Enlisted Groom* by Amy J. Fetzer. *The Forbidden Bride-to-Be* may be off-limits...but isn't that what makes the beautiful heroine in Kathryn Taylor's scandal-filled novel all the more tempting?

This November, Silhouette Desire is the place to live, love and lose yourself...to sensual romance. Enjoy!

Warm regards,

Joan Marlow Golan
Senior Editor, Silhouette Desire

Please address questions and book requests to:
Silhouette Reader Service
U.S.: 3010 Walden Ave., P.O. Box 1325, Buffalo, NY 14269
Canadian: P.O. Box 609, Fort Erie, Ont. L2A 5X3

MARY LYNN BAXTER
SLOW TALKIN' TEXAN

SILHOUETTE *Desire*®
Published by Silhouette Books
America's Publisher of Contemporary Romance

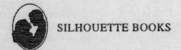

SILHOUETTE BOOKS

ISBN 0-373-76177-5

SLOW TALKIN' TEXAN

Printed in U.S.A.

Books by Mary Lynn Baxter

MARY LYNN BAXTER

A native Texan, Mary Lynn Baxter knew instinctively that books would occupy an important part of her life. Always an avid reader, she became a school librarian, then a bookstore owner, before writing her first novel.

Now Mary Lynn Baxter is an award-winning author who has written more than thirty novels, many of which have appeared on the *USA Today* list.

One

"**I** can't believe I'm doing this."

"For Pete's sake, it won't kill you. Not one time, anyway."

Ellen Saxton flashed her sister, Megan Drysdale, a put-out look. "It's easy for you to say. After all, *you* have a child."

"So?" Megan responded with a grin, which called marked attention to a dimple embedded in her left cheek.

Ellen gave her another look, followed by an unladylike snort. "So you know how to take care of one."

Meg was a part-time worker in the nursery in the small Baptist church she'd been active in for several years. According to her, the nursery was always short-handed and in need of substitute helpers.

"Think of this as just another adventure in your life," Meg said, her lips twitching.

"Oh, brother." Ellen rolled her eyes and watched her sister shift a precious two-year-old girl in her arms, then rock her. For sure, Meg had a knack with children.

Ellen felt a pang of envy for something she had missed in life and would more than likely never experience. By choice, she reminded herself quickly.

"Honestly, sis," Meg said, "it doesn't take a rocket scientist to change a baby's diaper."

"Well, it ought to," Ellen muttered more to herself than to Meg, while she turned her attention to the twenty-month-old baby boy in her charge.

His name was Matthew, and though he was a beautiful baby, even to her novice eyes, she hoped he wouldn't dirty his diaper while in her care. However, she feared that was wishful thinking. Besides, Meg wasn't about to let her get by without experiencing that side of motherhood.

Her next words confirmed that thought. "Just poke a finger inside his diaper and see if he's wet." Meg paused, then smiled a mischievous smile. "Or otherwise."

"It's the otherwise that has me concerned."

Meg laughed outright. "You really ought to loosen up a bit, you know."

"I wish I could."

"You can. Now that you're no longer married to that jerk, you have no reason to be strung out. Just pick up Matthew and cuddle him. You'll feel yourself mellow out."

Ellen shook her head. "Why bother him when he's content to sit on the floor and play with the toys?"

"Suit yourself," Meg said with a grin, "but if you're thinking what I think you are, you can think again."

"Now what would that be?" Ellen's tone was sugar-coated with innocence.

"Don't play the dumb-blonde with me. It won't work. We may only have two babies, but you're not cutting out."

Ellen gave her a sheepish look followed by a resigned sigh. "Give it a rest, okay? I gave my word, and though I wish I were home drinking a cup of coffee and reading the newspaper, I'm not going to leave you in the lurch."

"Praise the Lord."

"Having said that, you know you could handle them both. You're punishing me for something. I just haven't figured out what yet."

"Think of it as calling in a favor," Meg responded with a wink.

"Now that I can buy."

Meg shifted the suddenly squirming child to the other arm before narrowing her gaze back on Ellen. "I didn't mean that the way it sounded. When it's all said and done, I owe you much more than you owe me."

"Hey, we're not keeping score here." Ellen reached over and wiped the slobber off of Matthew's chin.

Meg chuckled. "See, you do know what you're doing."

"I wouldn't take that to the bank."

"Well, maybe your expertise does lie more in the workplace than in the homeplace, but—"

"But still, I'm not getting off the hook. Right?"

Meg grinned down at Matthew. "Right. But I'll concede that choosing a career over motherhood was the right thing for you. However, it's not too late for you to change your mind."

"I'm happy with my life as it is, thank you."

"I'm glad, now that I've lured you closer to me and my family."

Ellen gave a vigorous nod, agreeing with her sister wholeheartedly on that account. But the move from the booming town of Tyler, Texas, to this small, historic town of Nacogdoches hadn't been an easy one. Still, Ellen wasn't complaining. She'd found a prime location and opened her second coffee/gift shop, called Coffee, Anyone?

She was excited about that latest venture, despite the warnings that such a business might not take hold in a town of this size. She had merely ignored the naysayers and gone forward with enthusiasm.

To date, that positive attitude had paid off. According to the gossip hounds, her shop was now *the* place to go. Ellen was thrilled, of course, and hoped the excitement would last.

Opening a new business and getting it operational in just six months had been taxing, and she was exhausted. That was why she'd been reluctant to help Megan on Sunday, her only day off. While she'd done her best to finagle a way out, Meg wouldn't take no for an answer. Then again, the feeling that she owed

Meg more than she could ever repay had been a huge motivator.

Thank goodness there were only two babies in their care. Meg had chosen the little girl, because she was the most hyper. Matthew, on the other hand, had so far been content to remain on the floor and play with the toys that surrounded him.

Ellen glanced at her watch and breathed a sigh of relief. If all went according to plan, in thirty more minutes church would be over and her obligation ended. Her thoughts were interrupted by her sister's voice.

"I know this is probably a no-no, but have you heard from your ex?"

Ellen avoided looking at her sister, and when she spoke, her answer was succinct. "No."

"Oops. Did I hit a sore spot? I have a habit of putting my big foot in my mouth."

Ellen forced a smile. "That you do, sis dear. But in this case, you didn't. Besides, he doesn't want to talk to me any more than I want to talk to him. We're history."

"God, I hope so. You deserve to be happy, something that would never have happened if you'd stayed with him."

"Speaking of husbands, how's Ralph?"

"The same. Gone all the time," Meg admitted with brutal frankness.

Ralph was a truck driver who Ellen thought preferred being on the road rather than tending to responsibilities at home. Apparently Meg agreed, though she'd never voiced her displeasure before.

"How's his health?" Ellen asked, her concern growing.

"The doctor can't seem to get his diabetes under control. And his driving that truck all over the country doesn't help the situation."

"Maybe the doctor can get through to him."

"He won't listen. Besides, I don't know what we'd do if he did get off the road, though he's not getting the good hauls like he used to."

"Meggy, I sense something's going on that I need to know about."

"No more than usual. It's just that Kyle's seventeen and needs his dad around. It's all I can do to keep the bit in his mouth. I love him, but sometimes I could strangle him. And Ralph, too."

Ellen almost flinched visibly on hearing the pain and frustration in her sister's voice. Cutting another glance at Meg, she saw those emotions on her face, as well.

While Meg had never lost the weight after Kyle was born, at thirty-five she was still an attractive, brown-eyed brunette. But Ellen sensed that her sister was under more stress than she let on, suspecting the family was not only short on unity but funds, as well.

However, Ellen was reluctant to voice those thoughts. Meg was both proud and private, but when and if she needed help, hopefully she would ask for it.

Though they were as different in looks and personality as two sisters could be, they were close, having lost their parents within a year of each other—one to cancer and the other to a stroke. That tragedy had created a bond that would never be broken.

Suddenly Matthew let out a wail, jerking her back to the moment at hand. Shoving a strand of strawberry blond hair out of her face, Ellen got out of the chair, leaned over and hauled him into her arms.

Meg grinned. "He's quite a chunk, isn't he?"

"You can say that again. If I had to carry him around for any length of time, I think he'd break my arms."

"You'd get used to it."

"I doubt that." Then, to Matt, she said, "Hey, kid, mind your manners and stop wiggling."

"You might as well ask for a million dollars," Meg said. "Him being still ain't gonna happen."

"I guess I'd best check his diaper." Ellen's tone was resigned. "Maybe that's what's wrong with him."

"Probably."

Ellen gave Meg a pleading look. "I'll hold Miss Prissy if you'll change him for me."

"Not on your life. He's yours for the duration."

"I'll remember this."

Meg laughed. "I'm sure you will—for more reasons than one."

"Oh, all right, have your fun. I'm a big girl. I can take it."

"Go for it, sis."

Ellen made a face at Meg before she carried Matthew across the room to the changing station and laid him down. Immediately he started crying and flinging his arms and legs about.

"Hey, sweetie, hold your horses, okay? This won't take long, I promise."

Somehow Ellen managed to get his diaper, which was indeed wet, off. In fact, it was soaked. Much to her relief, that was all he'd done.

From behind, Ellen heard her sister chuckling. Without turning, she said, "Behave yourself and get your butt over here and help me."

"You don't need me. You're doing just fine."

"How can you say that when he's squirming so hard I can't get the clean diaper under him?" Ellen asked.

"You'll manage."

"Megan," Ellen said through clenched teeth, "I swear if this kid pees on me, I'll—" Suddenly she broke off with a loud cry as a stream of liquid shot up and landed first on her chin and then on her yellow silk blouse.

For a moment Ellen froze. Then she let out a loud cry of her own. "Yuk!"

"Uh-oh, looks like he had an accident." Meg's voice quivered with laughter. "I can't believe the little fellow did that."

"Yes, you can," Ellen spat, fighting to get the diaper under Matt and the tabs in place. Once that was done, she whipped around to face her sister, only to stop and stare at the doorway.

A man with a wide grin splayed across his face filled the space. That grin turned lazy as his eyes toured her body. Ellen flushed, conscious of the ugly stain front and center on her blouse.

Flustered and unnerved by this stranger's stare, which seemed to make fun of her ineptness, she snapped her eyes off him and back onto the still-squirming baby.

"Need any help?" he asked.

"Thanks, but no thanks," Ellen responded in a scoffing tone, thinking it unlikely that this rangy cowboy was any more adept at changing a diaper than she was. "Everything's under control."

"Are you sure about that?" he drawled.

"Yes, I'm sure," Ellen said coldly.

Megan stood and cleared her throat. "Uh, Ellen, this is Porter Wyman, Matthew's daddy."

Two

More mortified than she'd ever been in her life, Ellen stood transfixed and watched as Matthew's daddy, six feet of muscle and brawn, tipped his hat, then sauntered toward them.

The instant Matthew saw his daddy, he squirmed, waved his arms and grinned from ear to ear.

"Whoa, little boy." Ellen held on to him for dear life, fearing he was going to leap out of her arms.

"He's a handful, I'll admit," Porter said, reaching to take him from Ellen.

Feeling splotches of color invade her cheeks, Ellen kept her face averted. She had no idea what this man was thinking, but she could guess. All the more reason not to be on the receiving end of those brown eyes that reminded her of dark chocolate.

"Hey, son, you and me need to have a talk," Porter

said in a gravelly voice that sounded as if he could easily have been a drinking man.

Ellen knew better. He was in too good shape physically, especially his midsection. Even though it was disguised under a cotton shirt, she bet it would resemble an old-time washboard. Realizing the direction her thoughts had taken, her color heightened.

"Yeah, son, when we get home, we've got to talk about manners."

"I'll have to say, he pulled a boner," Meg chimed in, laughter threatening to bubble over.

"Shame on you." Porter gave his son a playful tug on the chin before transferring his gaze to Megan.

"How 'bout introducing me to your friend my son just assaulted?"

Ellen forced herself to look at her sister, then at Porter. They were having a good laugh at her expense, and she wanted to turn up her nose at them. But she knew that would make the situation worse for her. She kept her features devoid of emotion. Yet she couldn't help but bristle inside.

"Actually she's my little sister," Meg said with a devilish smile.

"Ah, I see. Well, does she have a name?"

"It'd be nice if y'all would stop talking about me as if I weren't in the room." Ellen heard the sharp primness in her tone, but she didn't care. To hell with both of them.

"That she does," Meg said, as if Ellen hadn't spoken. "Porter, meet Ellen Saxton."

Porter again tipped his Stetson, and his smile burgeoned, showing a row of perfect white teeth that added an extra dimension to his attractiveness. "Pleased to meet you."

"Same here," Ellen said, telling an outright lie.

"Sorry about the uh, accident," Porter said, his gaze narrowing on her.

Again Ellen wondered what was going on behind those incredible eyes, then mentally kicked herself for caring. It wouldn't bother her if she never saw him or his kid again. She just wished he would take Matthew and leave. Her patience with this entire episode was wearing thinner than a piece of rotten thread.

"That's okay," Ellen finally said. "It happens with babies."

Porter's gaze held steady. "So you know."

"Not from experience." Ellen's response was stiff.

"Ah, that's too bad."

That's your opinion, she wanted to lash back. But she didn't; she curbed her tongue, not giving a damn what he said or thought.

"I'm not so sure about that," Meg said with a chuckle. "My sister's not the motherly type."

Porter shifted his eyes back to Ellen. "Well, anyhow, tell the cleaners to send me the bill for your blouse."

"That's not necessary," Ellen said. "It's no big deal."

"I insist," Porter said, a hint of steel in his tone, though his pleasant demeanor didn't change.

Ellen shrugged. "Fine."

Porter looked at her for another long moment, then turned to Meg. "So how are things with you and your family?"

"I guess all right."

An eyebrow quirked. "You don't sound so sure."

"Thanks for asking."

"You bet," Porter said.

Ellen noticed how cleverly her sister had side-stepped the question. She swallowed a sigh, wishing Meg would confide in her, unable to squelch the feeling that something was not quite right with Meg and her family.

"We're outta here."

Porter walked over and reached for Matthew's diaper bag. "Much obliged for taking care of my kid."

Later Ellen was sure it was just her imagination, but she could have sworn his eyes lingered on her a bit longer than necessary.

After he'd gone, silence filled the room, though not for long. The little girl's parents came for her, but once they were gone and the sisters were finally by themselves, Meg laughed outright, pointing at the dark stain on Ellen's blouse.

Ellen glared at her. "If you don't put a lid on it, I just might strangle you."

Meg laughed that much harder.

"Megan, I'm warning you!"

"All right, I'm sorry."

"No you're not, not in the least," Ellen retorted, though she was having a hard time keeping a straight face herself.

"All I can say is, you got christened whether you wanted to or not."

"Funny."

"I thought so."

"You're making a big deal out of nothing. And so, sister dear, I'm leaving." Ellen's tone was huffy as she made her way to the door, but not before grabbing her purse and slinging it over her shoulder. She'd begun to smell herself and feared she was about to be sick to her stomach.

"Hey, hold your horses," Meg cried.

Ellen stopped and swung around. "Why? I upheld my end of the bargain. I helped you out. Now I'm going home."

"Aren't you the least bit curious about Porter Wyman?"

"Should I be?"

"Yeah, as a matter of fact you should."

"Why?"

"I figured that was obvious."

"Well, you figured wrong."

"God, sis, I know you're divorced, but I didn't think you were dead."

Ellen counted to ten. "I hardly think my lack of curiosity about your friend qualifies me as a cadaver."

"Well, you know what I mean."

"Nope, sorry, I don't."

"Look, I know you're not still carrying a torch for your ex."

"Megan, what's this all about? I'm tired. I stink. I want to go home. *I want a bath.*"

Meg laughed again. "You stink, huh?"

"Boy, you're sure full of piss and vinegar today. Too bad Ralph's not home to take some of that starch out of you."

"We're talking about you, not me." Meg paused, grinning again. "I saw the way Porter looked at you."

In spite of herself, Ellen flushed, then wished she could reach her own backside so she could kick it. "And just how was that?"

"You know."

Ellen's lips thinned. "No, I don't know, and what's more, I don't care. For heaven's sake, Meg, the man's married with a baby. If he was looking at me, then he's a cad."

"Oh, but you're wrong. He has every right to look at you, or any other woman he pleases. You see, he's not married."

Ellen frowned. "Then whose baby is that?"

"His."

"His, but—" Ellen clamped her lips shut. This was a subject she wasn't interested in pursuing, though Meg certainly was. Maybe if she indulged her, then she could go home and get that coveted bath.

"Right after Matt was born, Porter's wife, Wanda, hauled ass."

Ellen's mouth flopped open. "You're kidding."

"I wouldn't kid about something like that. The scandal stood this town on its ear."

"What made her do such a thing?"

Meg lifted her shoulder in a shrug. "Gossip had it she couldn't handle motherhood or being tied down, which, in my book, translates into not wanting to be married."

Ellen shook her head, trying to take it all in. "You never know what goes on behind closed doors. Maybe there were reasons why she didn't want to stay married to him.''

Meg snorted. "I don't believe that for a second. She was just trailer trash when they tied the knot, and even though she married money, she couldn't break that trashy mold."

"You mean he has money?"

"Tons."

"Could've fooled me. He looked like he shops at the nearest Goodwill. Not that there's anything wrong with that," Ellen hastened to add, "if that's the best you can do."

"Around here, jeans and boots hardly qualify as Goodwill duds."

Ellen sighed. "Whatever."

"Porter's probably the richest man in town."

"That blows my mind."

Megan grinned. "Besides being rich, he's the most sought after bachelor in the county."

"Good for him."

"Still not interested?"

"Not in the least."

"Sure about that?"

"Deadbang sure."

"He's a damn good catch."

"Then let someone else go fishing."

"Cute."

Ellen gave her a cheeky grin. "Thought so myself."

"Of course, I've been told he's sworn off women, that he's only interested in raising his son."

"Kudos to him."

"Heavens, sis, you're a hard nut to crack. Aren't you the least bit interested in how he got all his money?"

"No, but I'm sure you're going to tell me anyway."

"Right."

"Then get it over with," Ellen said in a bored tone.

"He owns a huge farm equipment store, plus thousands of acres of prime ranch land."

"So he's a real East Texas cowboy."

"And what's wrong with that?"

"Down girl. Nothing's wrong with that. He's just not my type, even if I were interested in a man, which I'm not."

"I hope that creep you were married to hasn't turned you off men for good."

"Maybe not for good, but certainly for now."

"You're too young to have that attitude."

"That's easy for you to say, Meggy. You didn't live with Samuel."

Meg's face sobered along with Ellen's. "I know it was bad, but—"

"Let's just say that it was far worse than even you knew."

Meg's face turned pale. "He...he didn't physically abuse you, did he?"

"No, but—" Ellen broke off. "Look, Samuel's history, and I'd rather not dredge up the past." She forced a lame smile. "Especially when I smell like stale pee."

Meg giggled, then cocked her head to one side. "I can understand that, although Kyle only showered me one time that I can remember." She paused. "Seriously, you wouldn't consider going out with Porter if he were to ask you?"

"Read my lips. No, Megan!"

Meg backed up and held up her hands. "Okay, okay. I get the picture."

"I'm not sure you do. I don't care how much money the man has, or how much land. He's not my type. Besides, I have my shop, and that's enough for me. I need to heal emotionally. Only time will tell if I can handle another relationship."

"You're right. Sorry, I got out of line. But you can't blame me for trying. I really like Porter, and I really like you, so—" Meg broke off with a grin.

"So it ain't gonna happen. Babies and cowboys are not my thing and never will be."

And with that Ellen flashed her sister a saccharine sweet smile and walked out the door.

Three

Ellen couldn't control the smile that spread across her face, even though she still smelled like a dirty diaper. Instead of going home as planned, she'd gone to the shop.

Every time she walked inside her domain, a giddy feeling washed through her. This Sunday afternoon proved no exception.

She didn't know why she had changed her mind and come here. Maybe it was because she had wanted to prove something to herself. Even though she didn't have the two things in her life that most women had or coveted: a husband and a child, she was nevertheless a fulfilled woman.

Envy of others' situations was utter nonsense, she knew. Yet she couldn't seem to toss such feelings aside as easily as she once had, especially after today and her experience in the church nursery.

However, this morning had changed nothing, except to reenforce the fact that she had made the right decision in divorcing Samuel. Conceiving a child under those circumstances would have been a disaster.

Ellen perused the coffee shop, which was at the end of a building housing several antique shops, each unique in what it sold. Coffee, Anyone? carried that uniqueness a step further in that it had a small private courtyard attached, giving her customers the feeling of drinking and dining in an atmosphere rivaling that of an open-air French café.

She had made the most of that unusual outdoor setting by decorating it to the hilt with small tables and flowering potted plants. A wonderful fountain in the middle provided an extra touch.

The inside was no slouch, either. The shelves featured a wide range of prepackaged gourmet foods, gift items from stationery to small wedding presents, and custom gift baskets.

Of course, the drawing card was the coffee. Virtually every popular gourmet brand, with frozen cappuccino the most sought after, was served. In addition, finger sandwiches, salads and delectable desserts were on the menu.

In just six months, this second Coffee, Anyone? was as successful as the larger one she'd left behind in Tyler. A friend, who was also a savvy businesswoman, was the manager there now.

But her success in Nacogdoches hadn't been without its price. Ellen was bone-weary from working day and night to get to this stage. There had been bumps along the way, bumps that still hadn't been smoothed out. The equipment was one of her biggest concerns. She'd had trouble with some of the machines since day one, mainly because they were used models. Soon she hoped to replace them with new ones.

She'd been fortunate with her help, which was a big hurdle to overcome. In the beginning, Meg had pitched in and helped sort through boxes. Before opening, she'd hired a college girl who so far had been good and dependable. But for the most part, the business was her baby, and she loved every minute of nurturing it.

Thinking of it as "her baby" changed Ellen's expression from a smile to a forlorn one, her mind suddenly switching to the love she'd seen mirrored in Porter's eyes when he'd taken his son from her arms.

More than likely she would never experience that kind of love. Still, she told herself, that was out of choice, not necessity.

"So stop the pity party," she muttered aloud. Besides, pity parties weren't much fun alone.

Deciding she needed a cup of iced coffee to buck up her spirits and combat the climbing June heat, Ellen made an iced cappuccino in a paper cup so she could take it home with her.

Thirty minutes later, she was in her rented patio home, out of the shower and still sipping the iced coffee. While her mind remained a bit unsettled, at least she no longer smelled.

The memory of the incident in the nursery suddenly

brought on a smile, a smile that soon faded into sadness as a bout of intense loneliness struck her.

Before she could beat up on herself for wandering down that forbidden path, the phone rang. It was Meg.

"Didn't I just leave you?" Ellen asked, a teasing note in her voice.

"That you did," Meg responded.

"So, what's up?"

"Want to come to dinner? Before I left for church, I put a roast and all the fixings in the Crock-Pot. I should've asked sooner, but I forgot."

"Sounds tempting, but I'm not really hungry."

"Okay." Meg paused. "By the way, thought any more about Porter?"

"No, dammit, I haven't. There's nothing to think about."

"Hey, don't jump on me. I was just hoping."

"Well, hope in another direction. Like I told you, it ain't gonna happen."

"You're making a big mistake."

"Well, it's not the first one, and it sure as hell won't be the last one, either."

"You're impossible."

"You're hard-headed."

"I guess that makes us sorta even."

"So I'll talk to you later, Meggy dear."

With that, Ellen placed the receiver back on the hook, though she continued to stare at it. One thing about Meg, she knew which buttons to push. If she could get her hands on her sister, she would strangle her, and cheerfully, too.

Porter Wyman.

She didn't want to think about him. She didn't want to think about *any* man, not in a personal way. Generic thoughts about him and his baby were harmless. But dwelling on the man himself was not a good idea.

Still, Ellen's mind wouldn't let go, even though she straightened the house with a vigor she should have reserved for the shop. Come morning, she had a storeroom full of "pretties" to unpack and enter on the computer.

What was there about the rancher turned businessman that had snagged her attention in the first place? Admittedly, he was good-looking in a rugged sort of way, with his dark hair, chocolate eyes and athletic build. But since her divorce, she'd run across several men who fit that mold. She hadn't given any of them the time of day, much less anything else. She wasn't going to give Porter anything, either.

Attractive or not, a slow-grinning man who had an infant to raise wasn't for her. She doubted he ever would be, though she was quick not to classify herself as a cold-hearted career woman.

For now, she was into treating herself well. That was what the shop was all about. It was something she had created, something she'd accomplished on her own. Before, during the Samuel years, everything had been done according to *his* wishes.

He had been a control freak as well as a perfectionist. A perfectionist herself, she had thought she and Samuel would be a match made in heaven. She found out quickly just how wrong she'd been. Their union had turned into a match made in hell.

Maybe she would marry again, and maybe she

would even have a child, just not anytime soon. The scars left from her two-year marriage were too raw.

Since she didn't believe in wallowing in self-pity and crying over what might have been, she had picked up the broken pieces of her life and gone on. She was free to go about her life without fear of Samuel's unwanted presence.

That was the main reason she didn't want to get involved with another man, especially someone like Porter Wyman. Besides, she didn't have a clue how to care for a child. No doubt he'd gotten that message today.

Thrusting aside the image of Porter's lazy grin and gait as he came toward her, Ellen leapt off the couch, grabbed her purse and headed to the door.

The ringing phone stopped her, but only momentarily. "Not this time, Meg," she said, walking out the door. She was going back to the office to work.

She'd had her fill of her sister and that cowboy for one day.

"Like that, huh?"

Matthew's laughter rang out as Porter tossed him once again into the air.

"That's all, son. Daddy has to go to work."

"Anything special you want me to do today?"

Porter gave his son a smack on the cheek before turning to face his housekeeper and nanny, Bonnie Temple. She was an attractive, dark-haired woman with expressive green eyes.

Although she was forty-five years old, ten years his senior, she didn't look it. Her build was slight and her hair was minus any gray, or any that he could see, anyway. But then, what did he know about hair color? His ex, Wanda, had changed hers with the seasons.

When Wanda had left him, he'd hired Bonnie immediately; she had come highly recommended. He hadn't been sorry one day. She was great with Matthew, having reared three children of her own. Because she was a widow, she also had the necessary freedom and flexibility to care for him and Matt.

She was smiling at him now, waiting for his answer.

He smiled back. "Nope, can't think of a thing, except to take care of my boy here."

"That goes without saying."

Porter handed Matthew to her.

"Is steak all right for dinner?" Bonnie asked.

"I might not be home till late, but I'll let you know."

Porter noticed the frown that suddenly doused Bonnie's smile, but he didn't comment on it. Not only did she love to clean house, but she loved to cook. If he didn't have so much land and so many cattle to care for, he'd have to watch his waistline.

A few minutes later, Porter climbed into his fancy truck and headed toward the store, knowing he should be in the pasture mending that south fence. He would take care of that tomorrow if Joe, his foreman, didn't get to it.

With the business and the ranch, there never seemed to be enough hours in the day, especially because he always tried to make time for Matt. That was a must. His son would always come first, no matter what.

His son.

What a perfect thought on a perfect summer day, he told himself, as he swung into his parking slot at the store a short time later.

"Morning."

Porter climb out of the cab and watched as his friend and manager, George Hays, limped toward him. George was another person he couldn't imagine doing without. In his late fifties, George had been injured in 'Nam. Even with a badly mangled leg, he was a workhorse. The store was an awesome responsibility, and George handled it and the customers like a pro.

But unlike him, George needed to watch his waistline. In fact, he needed to go on an outright diet, Porter thought, worried that his friend might have a stroke. Although he didn't drink beer, George had the proverbial beer-belly.

"Don't say a damn word," George grumbled as they walked into the building and made their way to the coffee room at the back.

"I don't recall opening my mouth."

George glared at him before filling a cup with coffee. "But you were thinking it."

Porter grinned, then filled his own cup. "Hell, don't climb all over me. You know what you have to do. The doctor's already warned you."

"Yeah, yeah."

Porter shook his head, sat down at the round table and remained silent, while George followed suit.

"So what else is on your mind?"

Porter narrowed his gaze. "What makes you think there's anything?"

"'Cause I know you."

"You old coot, you just *think* you know me."

"Let's have it."

Porter lifted the cup and blew on the liquid, his eyes on George. After taking a sip, he said, "I met a woman."

George harrumphed.

"I'm serious."

"That's what I'm afraid of."

"What's that supposed to mean?"

"After Wanda, I was under the impression you'd sworn off women."

"I had. I *have,* I mean."

"You can't have it both ways." George didn't bother to hide his sarcasm.

"You're an ass, you know that?"

George chuckled. "Okay, you've got my curiosity roused. Who is she?"

Porter told him, then listened as laughter bent George double. "So Matt christened her real good. And in the church, too. What a hoot!"

"That he did, and that it was."

George chuckled again. "So what's next?"

"Don't know."

And he didn't. After Wanda left him, he had indeed sworn off women. So far, he'd kept that vow. But after meeting Ellen Saxton, he was having second thoughts—big time. Under the circumstances, what man wouldn't? He was convinced she was the prettiest woman he'd seen in a long time, with her strawberry blond hair, periwinkle eyes and a body that made him sit up and take notice whether he wanted to or not.

"What do you mean, you don't know?"

"I'd like to see her again, but she's as uptight as she is pretty. Unfortunately."

"Too bad. Them uptight women are hell to handle."

"You're telling me. I seem to have a knack for getting involved with prissy, independent women."

"Then leave her alone."

"Afraid I can't do that."

"Why the hell not? If you're hankering to play again, this town's full of easy women." George winked. "If you know what I mean."

"I know what you mean, all right. But there's something about this particular one that's special, that intrigues me."

"And you're hell-bent on finding out what that something is."

"You got it."

George stood and peered down at his boss. "Want some advice?"

"Nope."

"I'm gonna give it anyway."

"Figured you would."

"No matter how intrigued you get, keep your damn fly zipped. Okay?"

Four

What was that noise?

Ellen paused just inside the back door of the shop and listened, certain she heard something, something that sounded very much like smothered giggles. Of course, that couldn't be. It was only a smidgen past eight-thirty in the morning. Her part-time helper, who was a college student, wasn't due in until around ten, opening time.

Yet Ellen heard the sound again. She frowned at the same time that her heart upped its beat. Could the noise be rats? God forbid. That thought panicked her more than an intruder.

Easing down her carryall and purse, she tiptoed toward the front of the shop, only to pull up short and stare, her mouth gaping.

Janis Waller, her employee, was going at it hot and

heavy with some young man. She had no idea who he was. His back was to her. Nonetheless, she could hear the sucking and moaning sounds resulting from their kissing and fondling. From where she stood, she could even see him squeezing one of Janis's breasts.

When she finally found her voice, Ellen snapped, "The party's over, kids."

If she had screamed fire, they couldn't have been more stunned. They broke apart instantly. Janis's hand flew to her mouth, while her eyes, wide and round, landed on Ellen.

"Uh, Ms. Saxton, I didn't expect—" she stammered.

"That's obvious."

Red stained the petite redhead's cheeks as she faced the young man. Though his back was still to Ellen, she·sensed he was as shaken as his girlfriend. His shoulders were as rigid as a block of wood, a block of wood that seemed suddenly familiar.

"Maybe you should introduce me to your friend," Ellen said with a coolness she was far from feeling.

The red stain in Janis's cheeks flared even more as the boy inched around. For a moment Ellen simply stared into his ashen face, trying not to show her shock and anger.

"Hello, Kyle."

"Hi, Aunt Ellen."

Another silence lasted for several heartbeats. Ellen broke it on a harsh sigh. "First off, why aren't you in class?"

Kyle, Meg's only child, was a senior in high school. By all accounts, he should have been in first period—unless he planned to cut classes altogether. From the looks of things, that was exactly what he planned.

If she hadn't come in when she had, would they have been on the floor making love? Kids!

"Are you going to tell Mother?"

"No, you are."

Though big and strong like his daddy, he seemed to wilt like an unwatered flower in the hot sun. "I...can't."

"Oh, yes, you can."

His features turned a sickly green. "She'll kill me."

"I doubt that, but she might want to."

Kyle's mouth turned down, giving it a sullen twist. "She's been on my case about everything lately."

"You should've thought of that before you pulled this little stunt." Ellen focused her attention on Janis. "What's your excuse?"

"I didn't think you'd catch us," the girl said with unexpected honesty. "I figured Kyle would be gone before you got here."

Ellen shifted her gaze back to her nephew. "So you weren't planning on playing hooky?"

"Nah."

Ellen didn't believe him for a minute, but she wasn't about to argue. She felt sorry for her sister. This wasn't the first trouble Kyle had been in, and it wouldn't be the last. Still, Meg was going to have a conniption fit. With her husband ill and on the road, this stunt would worsen an already volatile situation.

Ellen held out her hand. "The key, Janis."

What a mess, Ellen thought, as she took the key from the girl and slipped it into the pocket of her slacks. Janis Waller's parents were both wealthy and well-respected. She had met them at a party shortly after she'd arrived in Nacogdoches. The party had been in their home, and they had asked her to give their daughter a job. Janis needed something to keep her busy when she wasn't in class, they had told her.

Ellen could understand why now. But she had trusted Janis enough to give her a key in the event that she herself couldn't get there to open on time. Until now, the young woman had never given her a moment's hint that she was anything other than trust-worthy and reliable.

"When did you two become an item?" Ellen asked into the growing silence.

The kids looked at each other, then both shrugged. "Several months ago," Janis finally said.

"I see."

Janis fiddled with the collar of her blouse. "Are you going to fire me?"

"Don't you think I should?"

"Yes, ma'am," Janis said, lowering her head. "Only I wish you'd give me another chance." Her head popped up, and her eyes were pleading. "My parents'll kill me, too."

Ellen didn't bother to hide her disgust. "Cut the dramatics, both of you. While I'm certainly offended by your actions, I'm more upset that Kyle wasn't in school."

"I hate school," Kyle muttered.

"So did I," Ellen said coldly, "but I still went."

"You don't understand."

Janis looked at him, then reached for his hand. "Please, just go. Okay?"

"Yeah, I'm outta here."

He leaned over and kissed Janis full on the lips, as if to show Ellen that she didn't scare him. Ellen swallowed a sigh along with the urge to grab him, turn him over her knee and wallop the living daylights out of him. He was too old and too big for such antics.

Besides, he wasn't her kid. Meg and Ralph were responsible for her nephew's behavior, not she, thank goodness. However, she was worried. Kyle's armor of belligerence was a legitimate concern.

Once he was gone, Janis stared at the floor again before looking back up at Ellen. "I'm sorry. Really I am."

"I believe you."

"You do?"

Ellen smiled. "Yes."

"What about Kyle?"

"What about him?"

Janis hesitated, a frown marring her forehead. "He's been acting kind of squirrelly lately. I'm not sure what's going on."

"Me, either. But right now, you and I have work to do. There are six boxes to unpack. That's your job."

"Then I'm not fired?"

"No. I believe in second chances, but not third ones."

"Yes, ma'am."

* * *

Ellen ran a hand through her hair, and her palm came away moist. Damn, but it was hot, she thought even though the air conditioner was on as far as she dared turn it. The shop was still in the red, and she had to be careful.

What a day, and it wasn't over yet. The morning's escapade with Janis and Kyle had started her off on the wrong foot. Things had gone from bad to worse. When Janis started unboxing the freight, half of the items shipped turned out to be either wrong or damaged.

She'd been furious and still was. But there wasn't anything she could do about the problem except re-order, which took time.

Ellen glanced at her watch, noticing that closing time was only thirty minutes away. She had expected to hear from Meg sometime during the day; so far she hadn't. Apparently Kyle hadn't told her yet or she would have called demanding Ellen's side of the story.

Just how serious were Kyle and Janis? But how serious did kids nowadays have to be to make love? God, she hoped Janis wouldn't turn up pregnant. That thought sent a chill darting through her. At this moment, she didn't envy her sister having a teenager.

The Lord seemed to have known what he was doing when he hadn't given her a child.

The buzzer on the door sounded, drawing her attention away from her maudlin thoughts. She smiled at the customer, only to have that smile disappear. Mrs. Cavanaugh. What had she done to deserve this?

Ellen asked herself. Especially at the end of a hellish day?

"I'm glad I caught you," Ruth Cavanaugh said in her haughtiest tone.

"Me, too," Ellen lied, plastering a fixed smile on her lips.

This tall, horse-faced woman had been her cross to bear from the first day she'd opened the shop. She was one of the richest, but most miserable, women Ellen had ever met.

"This tea set I bought yesterday doesn't work."

"What's wrong with it?"

"It's the wrong color."

Ellen sighed and held on to her temper by a thread. "Would you like to get another one?"

"No. The other colors aren't right, either. Besides, for what it is, it's too expensive."

Bitch. Ellen's fixed smile broadened. "I'll be happy to credit your account."

"I want my money back."

"That's not my policy."

Mrs. Cavanaugh's watery-blue eyes—a perfect match for her watery-blue hair, Ellen thought cattily—hardened. "Then change your policy."

"Fine." Ellen opened the cash drawer and withdrew a hundred dollars in twenties. "Here's your money."

"Thank you." With that, Ruth Cavanaugh turned and marched out the door.

"Damn!" Ellen muttered, feeling her stomach churn.

Coffee, Anyone? couldn't afford many financial

hits like that one and survive. But maybe she'd saved her reputation by returning the money to the cantankerous old biddy.

Deciding her troubles just *had* to be over for the day, Ellen went into the back room, remembering a gift she hadn't wrapped. She had just climbed to the top rung of the ladder to get the right box when she heard the buzzer.

Wouldn't you know it!

If whoever had come in spent money, she wouldn't mind climbing down. But if the customer only wanted a cup of coffee, she would not be happy. Immediately Ellen chastised herself for that attitude. A two-dollar coffee customer today could return tomorrow and buy a fifty-dollar gift.

That thought sent Ellen scrambling down the steps and into the front room. She'd barely cleared the door when she froze.

"Hi."

The last person she'd expected to see was Porter Wyman. Nevertheless, all six feet plus of him was leaning against the door, a smile strengthening the grin lines around his mouth and eyes.

Ellen cleared her throat and tried to collect herself. She didn't remember his being so big or so good-looking. Although he was dressed in worn jeans, a casual shirt and scuffed boots, attire she normally frowned on, she couldn't find fault with those clothes on him, a fact that didn't set well with her.

"Hi, yourself," she finally said, knowing she sounded out of breath. His presence had not only caught her off guard but flustered her, as well. Maybe

it was the way he was looking at her with those un-usual eyes, deep and mysterious.

"What can I do for you?" She couldn't imagine what he wanted in a shop like hers.

Porter grinned and pushed himself away from the door. "Nice place you've got here."

"You sound surprised," she responded, stiffening.

He shrugged. "Tell the truth, I didn't know what to expect. This isn't my thing, you know."

No kidding, she wanted to blurt out, but didn't. Not only would that be rude, but ugly to boot. But then, she was in an ugly mood, and his arrival had exac-erbated it. Even so, she was curious.

"So how's business?" he asked in an unhurried drawl, as if time was of no consequence.

"Fine." The stiffness in her body and voice was more noticeable than ever.

She knew he was aware of her discomfort; his mis-chievous smile said as much. "I hope I'm not keeping you from closing up."

"You're not," she said meaningfully, with a look at her watch.

"Good. That means you can finish and leave."

She blinked in confusion.

"I came to take you to dinner."

"I don't think that's a good idea," she said, taken aback.

"Why not?"

Ellen's heart was suddenly pounding much too fast. "I just don't."

His eyes traveled the length of her body, just as they had the Sunday she met him, which brought another flush to her face. She sensed she was in for a verbal fight. He didn't seem to be the type who took no for an answer, despite his laid-back demeanor.

"Okay."

"Okay?"

"Yeah, it's okay if you don't want to go to dinner."

Ellen opened her mouth, then snapped it shut.

"Later." He tipped his Stetson and walked out.

Five

Ellen sipped a glass of iced green tea as she stretched out on the chaise longue on her patio. She shouldn't have come home so early, but she had felt the need to get away from the shop for more reasons than one.

Thank goodness the days were getting longer, which meant more daylight to enjoy her home and its lovely surroundings. She couldn't take credit for the tiny, well-manicured yard, with its splattering of different colored annuals and tallow trees, but she *could* enjoy it.

Not sure she or her business would thrive here, she had put off buying a home. Yet she couldn't bear the thought of living in an apartment complex, where doors slammed at all hours and the neighbors' voices carried through the walls.

When a realtor she had contacted found this patio

home for rent, she'd snapped it up. She hadn't been sorry, especially since it was new; she was its first occupant.

A bird chirped, and a squirrel sprang from one flimsy tree branch to another. All the beauty, plus the soothing taste of the tea, should have relaxed her. It didn't. Her insides were still coiled tightly.

She still hadn't heard from Megan, which meant Kyle hadn't yet confessed his misadventure. What if he didn't? If not, what should she do? Her instinct told her that she had to tell her sister, but the thought of tattling on Kyle left a bad taste in her mouth.

Nevertheless, he'd been in *her* shop with *her* employee when he should have been at school. Even though she wasn't a parent, Ellen knew that was a precedent that couldn't get started.

But Kyle skipping school apparently wasn't the only problem in the Drysdale household. She just wished Meg would confide in her. Actually she wished a lot of things.

She wished she had never met Porter Wyman, for one thing. She wished he hadn't come to her shop today. She wished she didn't give a damn one way or the other. That was really what had her mind in a tizzy. He couldn't have showed up at a worse time. Timing, however, wasn't the problem. Even if everything had been going great, his mere presence would have set her off.

Ellen frowned as she took another sip of tea. He was trouble, the kind of trouble she should avoid at all cost. She was committed to pleasing herself for a change and not a man. That had been the reason behind turning down his dinner invitation. But dammit, she was drawn to him and didn't have a clue why.

The peal of the phone drew her thoughts back to the present. With a grateful sigh, she reached for the cordless on the table beside her.

It was Meg, and she sounded upset. Kyle. Had he finally fessed up?

"What are you doing?" Meg asked in a forlorn voice.

"Drinking tea."

Silence.

"Meggy, a glass is waiting for you."

"I feel bad about bothering you."

"Stop it!"

"I know, but—"

"Is Ralph still gone?"

"Yes. He called and said he won't be home for several more days."

"Why don't you come over?"

"Not after the day you've had."

"So Kyle told you."

"He did, and I nearly killed him."

"He said you would. But try to look on the bright side. Bad as it was, it could've been worse."

"I'm not buying that," Meg said. "I can't believe he pulled such a stunt in your place and with your helper. Of all the girls in this town—"

"It is a coincidence, I'll admit. But stranger things have happened. Somehow it'll work out, but only if you don't let it fester, meaning we need to talk."

"If you're sure I won't be—"

"Oh, for crying out loud. Just get your butt over here."

Fifteen minutes later, a swollen-eyed Megan joined her on the patio. After giving her sister a big hug, Ellen didn't say anything until Meg had drunk half a glass of tea.

"I'm listening."

Megan's lower lip trembled.

"Hey, whatever's going on in your life can't be that bad. I've never seen you like this, not even when Mom and Dad died."

Megan sniffed, then gave Ellen a watery smile. "I don't think I've ever been like this. I think—no, I know—my nerves are shot."

"Have you talked to your doctor?"

Meg nodded.

"And?" Ellen persisted.

"He gave me something, only—"

"You're not taking it."

"I haven't so far."

"That's stupid."

"Maybe, but you didn't take anything when you went through your divorce."

"What I did or didn't do has nothing to do with you. Anyway, who says I didn't take anything?"

Megan's eyebrows shot up. "Did you?"

"Sure did. Something to make me sleep, actually."

"Well, that's different. What I have is an antidepressant."

"So take the damn thing."

"I keep thinking I'll get it together and snap out of my funk."

"What's really going on, Meggy?"

"It's Kyle and Ralph."

Ellen's heart lurched. "Ralph? You mean you two are having trouble?"

"Yes and no."

"That's clear as mud."

Meg smiled briefly.

"Quit stalling," Ellen said, an impatient note in her voice.

"His diabetes is playing havoc with his kidneys. If the problem gets any worse—and it could, with him bouncing in that truck—I'm afraid he'll get laid off. I've already told you, he's not getting any of the lucrative hauls."

"Do you think the boss is trying to get rid of him?"

"Probably. And that's not all. Our finances are in terrible shape."

"I have an answer to that."

"So do I," Meg said. "Go to work."

"I'll hire you, starting tomorrow."

"Thanks, but no thanks. I'm not cut out for your profession. I'm a farm girl, not a charm girl."

"Cute."

"I love you, and we're blood kin, but you have to admit, we're as different as two sisters could possibly be."

"True, but that's what makes us special."

Meg's smile brightened. "I'm glad you still feel that way, especially after the stunt Kyle pulled."

"We'll get back to him later. Before we leave the subject of you and Ralph, what does he say about you going to work? I know in the past he's been against it.''

"Still is. In fact, he had a fit when I told him what I wanted to do.''

"He'll get over it.''

"You kidding? He'll probably have a stroke.''

"He's as possessive in his way as Samuel was in his.''

"Ralph's a redneck. Samuel's a jerk.''

Ellen laughed. "You won't get any argument from me. So what are you going to do?''

"Don't know. I'm still thinking about it.''

"Well, the offer to help at the shop is always open. The little twit who's working for me now won't be there long.''

Meg groaned. "Speaking of Janis brings us back to my son.''

"I'm glad *he* told you.''

Meg's gaze pinned her. "Would you, if he hadn't?''

Ellen sighed. "Probably, though I would rather have had a root canal.''

At first Meg looked as if she hadn't heard right; then she laughed outright. Ellen was glad to see the strained expression disappear from her sister's features, even if it was only temporarily.

"If I'd been in your shoes, I would've felt the same way.''

"So what's with Kyle? I have a feeling it's more than his involvement with Janis.''

"It is. He's gotten in with the wrong crowd at school.''

"Tell me he's not into drugs?"

"Not as far as I can tell. But then, I'm not up on the signs."

"Well, you'd best get up on them," Ellen said. "ASAP."

"You're right, but with Ralph in the shape he's in, I guess I've had my head buried in the sand."

"It's not too late to dig out. Janis is really a fine girl, from a fine home, but you don't want any out-of-wedlock children to worry about on top of everything else."

Meg turned wild-eyed. "God forbid that should happen."

"Well, it can," Ellen retorted. "In a heartbeat. Probably would have this morning if I hadn't come in when I did."

"Oh, Lordy, don't tell me that. Just the thought makes me sick."

"I wouldn't think the answer is getting sick but rather in getting tough."

"I did that. Only time will tell if it takes."

Ellen didn't ask for the details concerning Meg's altercation with her son. It didn't matter, as long as they had reached an understanding. She prayed that they had.

"Until you decide what to do about working, I'll be glad to loan you some money." Ellen waited for Meg's response with bated breath.

"I know, but I wouldn't take it."

"Why the hell not?"

"Because you're not in great financial shape yourself. Anyway, this is something we have to take care of on our own.''

"It's your call, but that and the job offer remain on the table.''

"Thanks,'' Meg muttered, tears gathering in her eyes.

"Ah, don't get mushy on me.''

Meg smiled. "Then let's change the subject. I'm tired of talking about me and my problems.''

"Well, you sure don't want to hear mine.''

"Yes, I do.''

"No, you don't.''

They looked at each other, then burst out laughing.

"I knew you should come over. Now we're both laughing like idiots.''

"Feels good, too.'' Meg leaned over and gave Ellen a spontaneous hug. "I'm so glad you're here. I just hope you'll stay. I know you really prefer living in Tyler, but—''

"Nacogdoches isn't so bad. Or at least it wasn't until…'' This time it was Ellen whose voice faded.

"Until what?'' Meg prodded, giving Ellen a pointed stare.

"Nothing.''

"Oh, no, you don't. Turnabout's fair play.''

"No, it isn't.''

"Until you met Porter. That's what you were going to say, isn't it?''

"Dammit, Meg!''

"Ah, so I was right.'' Meg grinned. "He's already in heat.''

Ellen lifted her head. "God spare me.''

"I'm right, aren't I?"

"It no longer matters. If the heat was on, I turned it off real quick."

"So he *did* ask you out?"

"Yes."

"Obviously you turned him down."

"Obviously."

"Oh, Ellen, how could you?"

"Easy. I just said no."

Meg cocked her head and grinned. "Aren't you the least bit interested? Before you say anything, don't you dare lie to me."

"I don't lie."

"Everybody lies."

"Okay, he *is* different, and I *am* curious."

"I knew it!"

"Simmer down. That doesn't mean anything. Besides, when I said no, he walked out as if he couldn't care less."

"Pooh! He cares. You just wait and see. He'll be back."

"It won't do him any good."

"You're lying again," Meg whispered.

Ellen's face turned scarlet, and for once she had no comeback.

Six

Porter grunted and groaned, but still the bolt wouldn't budge. "Dammit!"

"Hey, buddy, if you don't watch out, you're going to strip the threads on that thing."

Porter scooted out from under the tractor and glared up at his manager. "You think you can do any better?"

George grinned, seeming to take no offense at Porter's grumpy tone. "Nope, but then, I ain't gonna try. I figure that's what we hire those high-priced mechanics for."

"Only this is my rig, and so far those idiots haven't been able to fix it. And I'm tired of it breaking down every time I'm in the north pasture."

"Meaning you have to haul it back to the house."

"My point exactly."

George's grin widened as he shoved his hat back and rubbed a spot on his high forehead. "Get another one."

"This one's brand damn new." Porter's scowl deepened even as he scrambled to his feet.

"Well, all I can say is, they don't make things like they used to, and that includes farm equipment."

Porter brushed the loose debris off his jeans. "I won't argue with that."

"So want me to get one of the guys on it?"

"As in now. I want to mow this afternoon, before it rains again." Porter stared out one of the big windows in the shop and eyed a dark cloud. "Looks like I may be a day late and a dollar short as it is."

"Ah, in East Texas, you never know about the weather."

"You got any more sage advice for today?"

"Nah," George said with another grin before ambling back toward the showroom floor.

Porter, still scowling, went to the men's room and cleaned as much of the grease off his hands as he could. His nails would have to wait until he got home for the thorough cleaning they needed.

A few minutes later, George met him at the side door of the showroom, his forehead now deeply lined. "You got company."

"Who?"

"Earl Duke."

Porter's eyebrows shot up. Earl was his attorney, the one who had taken care of his divorce. "What does he want?"

"He didn't tell me, and I didn't ask."

Porter strode past George without another word and walked into his office. Earl, who was standing by the window, swung around. His wide features, made wider by a gray mustache that covered his upper lip and draped his mouth, were grim.

"You're the last person I expected to see this afternoon," Porter said, extending his hand.

"Duty calls," Earl said in his gruff voice, returning the handshake.

"What's up?"

"Mind if I sit down?"

"Sorry."

Earl lowered his heavy frame onto a leather chair in front of Porter's desk, then faced Porter, who sat on the edge of the desk. "What's so urgent that you had to see me in the flesh?"

"Wanda."

That word had the same effect as waving a red flag in front of an already mad bull. Fury locked further words in Porter's throat.

"She called and asked how Matthew was doing."

"What the hell does she care?"

"That's why I'm here."

"Go on," Porter said tightly, crossing his arms over his chest.

"She didn't ask to see him, but I know that's what she was hinting at."

"I'll see *her* in hell first."

"That's what I figured you'd say."

"She made her flea-infested bed. Let her lie in it and get eaten up."

"I expect that's exactly what she's doing."

"What happened to the love of her life, that creep she dumped Matt and me for?"

"He probably dumped her."

Porter snorted. "What did you tell her?"

"The truth, that Matt was fine."

"Bet she didn't drop it there."

"Actually she did. But she was crying, so I suspect we haven't heard the last from her, especially if that creep *has* dropped her."

"Well, she can't do a damn thing." Porter's eyes delved into Earl's. "Right?"

"You know the answer to that. She gave up all rights to her son."

"Then why did she call?"

"Who knows. Maybe she wanted to give you more grief. Or maybe she's having second thoughts and hankering to get Matt back."

"No chance."

"Let us pray."

Porter's heart clunked to his toes. "What the hell are you saying?"

"I'm saying that it's not impossible for some crazy judge to get a burr up his butt and end up ruling in Wanda's favor."

"Dammit, Earl, you'd better keep that from happening! She's not getting her hands on Matthew, you hear? Not ever again!"

Earl shuffled to his feet. "Settle down, boy. More than likely, we'll never hear from her again. But as your legal counsel, I'm obligated to keep you informed."

"Much obliged for making my day." Porter didn't bother to hide his sarcasm.

Earl half-smiled. "Anytime." Then, at the door, he turned and added, "Try not to worry. Maybe she was having PMS."

Porter snorted again. "She's an airhead, nothing more, nothing less."

"All the more reason to think her call means nothing."

"It had better not."

"If anything further develops, I'll handle it. I'll handle *her*."

"Just make her go away and stay away. That's all I ask. Meanwhile, find out where she is and what she's up to." Porter's hands curled into tight fists. "I want to know everything, even her bathroom habits."

"Consider it done."

The second Earl closed the door behind him, Porter struggled to get his next breath. He shouldn't have been surprised that Wanda had called, but he was. Women! Since he would never figure them out, the answer was to keep his distance.

Suddenly Ellen Saxton rose to the front of his mind. But then, she hadn't been very far away since he'd met her. A smile reshaped Porter's stiff lips, and he eased off the desk.

Thoughts of his ex weren't going to ruin the rest of his day. His broken tractor might, but not *her*. Wanda's call was nothing but a whim, something that she would get over. He wouldn't think about it another moment. Wasn't that what he paid Earl for? Keeping Wanda at bay was his job.

With that comforting thought, Porter made his way out of the office and said to George, "I'm outta here for the day."

"Oh, my gosh!"

Ellen was in the store room, unpacking merchandise, but she paused, hearing Janis's cry.

"Oh, my gosh!" Janis cried again.

What now? Ellen asked herself, dashing toward the front.

"Janis what on earth—" Further words deserted her as she took in the godawful mess in front of her.

The cappuccino machine had gone on the blink again. This time, though, it had done it up right. Slushy coffee was oozing out of the machine onto the floor faster than it could be cleaned up.

"Ugh!" Ellen cried, reaching for the plug, only to find that Janis had already pulled it.

"What happened?"

Janis shook her head, sending her long hair swishing around her face. "I don't know, Mrs. Saxton. Honestly. When I came around here to start cleaning up for the day, the machine was making an odd noise and this goop was all over the floor."

"Damn that critter! I should've know better than to buy anything secondhand." Ellen fought back the urge to give in to the tears of frustration that burned the backs of her eyelids.

When she'd first priced the new cappuccino machines in Tyler, she'd nearly had a stroke. She'd bought a used one for that shop, and so far it had performed like a champ. This one had been nothing but trouble from day one, though.

However, this mess was the worst yet. Thank God there weren't any customers in the shop. Since it was near closing time, hopefully the shop would remain deserted.

"Let's get busy. We don't have any choice except to clean it up."

"Uh, did you forget?" Janis asked, shifting from one foot to the other, her face devoid of color.

"Forget what?"

"That I have to be in class in ten minutes."

"Perfect."

"I can always cut class," Janis said, brightening. "I don't mind."

"Oh, but I do."

Janis's mouth turned down.

"Get going. I'll take care of this. It won't take long."

"Are you sure?"

"I'm sure. Get your things and get to class."

Still, Janis hesitated, a troubled look on her face.

"It's okay," Ellen said, forcing a smile. "I'll have this done in no time."

Janis wanted to argue; that was obvious in the stubborn twist to her mouth. But she didn't. Instead she muttered, "All right. I guess I'll see you tomorrow."

Once she was alone, Ellen grabbed some towels from under the counter, dropped to her knees and spread the cloths over the liquid. That was when the buzzer sounded.

"Oh, brother," she said under her breath.

No doubt whoever it was would be sure to want a cup of frozen cappuccino.

"Yo, anybody home?"

That voice! She would know it anywhere, even though she'd only heard it a couple of times. Meg was right. Porter had returned. With her heart threatening to pound out of her chest and her face fire-engine red, Ellen struggled to her feet, a difficult task, what with the coffee-scented slush underfoot.

"Good God, woman!"

Without turning around, Ellen knew he was behind her. Worse, her butt was in the air.

Damn this machine for breaking down. *Damn him!*

"Is that all you have to say?" she snapped.

Porter chuckled. "Now that you mentioned it, no. That's *not* all I have to say."

Sitting back on her haunches, Ellen twisted her head around and glowered at him over her shoulder. As she suspected, his eyes were focused on her derriere.

"Mmm, nice."

That did it. She forced herself upright and faced him, still glowering. "There's nothing nice about this mess!" she snapped, choosing to ignore the sexual connotation.

"I wasn't referring to the mess."

"Well, you should've been. Otherwise, you're way out of line."

"A line I'm willing to cross anytime."

"Go to hell."

Ellen knew she was overreacting, but she couldn't seem to stop herself. He was the last person she wanted to see. Or was he? Maybe that was what she was in such a stew over. She wanted to see him, only she didn't want to admit it.

He grinned, then moved away from the counter where he'd been leaning. "How 'bout I fix your machine instead?"

That unexpected comment took her aback. "You'll fix it?"

He shrugged. "Why not?"

"Can you?"

"It's a machine, isn't it?"

"Yes, but I doubt it's one you're familiar with."

He chuckled again, which made him sound and look too damn sexy. It wasn't fair. She didn't want to be attracted to this man.

"Doesn't matter. When I set my mind to it, I can fix most anything."

"Well, have at it."

"Step aside."

"What I'd like to do is throw the damn thing out the back door."

Porter gave her a keen look, though the corners of his mouth still held traces of a smile. "Relax. It's going to be okay. Trust me."

"Sure."

He laughed again. "Go lock the door, why don't you?"

"Are you trying to get rid of me?"

"Yep."

In spite of herself, Ellen smiled. "Thought so."

She felt his attention follow her all the way to the front, knowing that once again those incredible eyes were focused on her rear. Now, however, the anger she'd felt earlier had turned into a hollow sensation in the pit of her stomach.

Oh, boy, Ellen thought, that would never do.

After she had locked the door and returned to the counter, she realized his gaze was still on her. Flustered, she said in a quarrelsome tone, "So what are you waiting on?"

"Nothing. I'm finished."

"You mean it's fixed?"

"As in ready to make coffee."

Ellen's mouth dropped. "But how—I mean—"

"You really want to know the details?"

"No, not unless it's something that I could fix if it should go berserk again."

"You can't, and it won't. At least, not that particular problem."

"Er...thanks. What do I owe you?"

"Dinner."

Ellen swallowed as he came near her. "What if I'm not hungry?"

"That's okay. I'll eat, and you can watch."

"You don't give up, do you?"

"Not when I want something."

She decided not to pursue that statement. And if she ever wanted to get rid of him, she might as well have dinner and draw the line in the sand. "I'll get my purse."

"Won't need it."

"I'm treating, remember?"

"Only if you eat."

"That doesn't matter."

Porter raised his hands, that seemingly perpetual grin on his face. "Fine with me. I'm a liberated man."

That was very much what she was afraid of.

Seven

Instead of the food on his plate, Porter wanted to eat *her*. The entire time they had been at the restaurant, he'd toyed with his food and watched her. His gut twisted. What was wrong with him? He was behaving like a lovesick idiot who had never been with a woman.

At some point, everyone did something idiotic, he reminded himself. Apparently this evening was his time. But if he didn't get a grip soon, Ellen would probably toss some of the salad she was pushing around her plate in his face.

An unreleased smile spread through him. Talk about creating a commotion in this town—now *that* would do it. It would give those rich, lavender-haired ladies who camped in her shop something to talk about.

Still, Porter couldn't heed his own warning; he kept staring at her. Despite the delicate circles under her eyes and the mussed-up look to her lovely hair, she was absolutely fetching.

Feeling his loins stir, he shifted his position at the same time that he tore his eyes away from her. If he'd kept on, his gaze would have settled on her breasts, their roundness accented by the silk blouse she wore.

Silk.

Ah, that fit her to a tee. That smile inside itched to break out as he thought of how he was dressed.

Denim.

That fit *him* to a tee. Silk and denim—as different as two fabrics could be. But then, they were as different as two people could be, which made the chase that much more interesting.

Porter made himself concentrate on the surroundings. To continue dwelling on her breasts and how it would feel to cup their softness in his big calloused hands was suicidal and not likely to happen. Teasing himself with such a thought merely added to his physical misery.

Damn, he guessed he was just horny. But this woman was definitely not the type who would warm his bed just for the fun of it.

The café was not crowded, he noted; only two other couples were there. It wasn't fancy, either, but the food was delicious, only they weren't eating it.

"How's your baby?"

The husky timbre in Ellen's voice drew him back around. If she could have read his thoughts, she would have thrown the entire plate of food at him. "Matthew's fine."

"Did you think I didn't remember his name?"

She sounded affronted, which was his fault. For a moment it riled him to think that she might have forgotten his son's name.

"No," he lied.

Ellen didn't respond. Instead she lowered her head and fiddled with her dinner.

This liaison wasn't working out as planned. He put down his fork. "You're sorry you came, aren't you?"

Her head jerked back up, and her rounded eyes locked on him. "Are you sorry you asked me?"

He laughed. "Okay, have it your way. Not for a minute."

"I haven't been very good company."

"You haven't eaten your food, either."

Ellen blinked, calling his attention to her dark, thick lashes. "You haven't, either."

He shoved his plate aside, suddenly conscious of the slight discoloration under his nails. His hands were clean, though; hell, he'd scrubbed them until they were almost raw. The stains would have to wear off. In contrast, Ellen's nails were perfectly manicured.

"I guess I wasn't as hungry as I thought," he said, hating the notion that such a little thing as his nails bothered him. Heretofore, he hadn't given a damn about how he dressed or anything associated with vanity. People could take him as he was or not at all. To think she might have disturbed that complacency disturbed *him*.

"I'm too tired to eat," Ellen said at last.

"Well, your cappuccino machine's fixed, anyway."

That brought a smile. "I still can't believe you repaired it with so little effort."

"Gadgets are my thing."

"They're sure not mine."

A silence fell between them as the waitress took their plates and refilled their glasses.

"So are you involved with anyone?"

Ellen gave him a startled look. "You certainly don't waste time."

"Or mince words."

"That's really none of your business."

"It is if I want to see you again."

Color invaded her cheeks, and she gave him another startled look. "Sorry, but I'm not interested."

"Is it just me?"

"No."

"I see."

"Men aren't high on my priority list."

"Mind telling me what is?"

"Me."

Porter pitched back his head and laughed, bringing stares to their table.

The flush on Ellen's face deepened even as she said, "That sounded awful, didn't it?"

"Truthful, and I like that."

"You're just being tactful."

Porter cocked his head. "Wrong. When you get to know me better, you'll learn that being tactful is *not* my thing."

She let that slide, which made him want to push that much harder. He knew he was crazy, but he wanted to see this woman again.

Maybe if he had a few beers and a good lay, he'd get over this continual and growing urge to take her.

"Who takes care of Matthew?"

"I have a live-in housekeeper. Her name is Bonnie, and she's a jewel."

"You're lucky. People like that are hard to come by."

"I know. Matthew's crazy about her, too."

"You seem crazy about him."

"You sound surprised."

"A lot of men wouldn't dare assume sole responsibility for a baby."

"Well, I'm not most men."

"I believe that."

"So you've been filled in on all the gory details?"

Ellen looked away briefly, then back again. He caught her gaze and held it for a moment. He saw confusion and uncertainty in their depths.

"Actually I haven't. Meg told me your wife left, that's all."

"Well, if that's all she told you, then she gave you a real short version of a long and nasty story."

"I'm sorry."

"Yeah, me, too, but it's water under the proverbial bridge now."

"Does Matthew see his—" Ellen stopped and looked away as though embarrassed.

"Mother. It's okay to ask about her."

"No, it isn't. That's none of my business."

He rubbed his chin. "Doesn't bother me. The answer is not no, but hell no. She gave him up, lock, stock and barrel."

"I can't imagine any woman doing such a thing."

"If you were to meet her, you could."

Ellen didn't respond to that, and he didn't expect her to. Wanda was the last person he wanted to discuss with this woman, at least this evening. Wanda, having called about Matthew that very day, had reopened a wound that he'd thought was closed.

"So what about *your* ex?"

She looked away, then back at him. "He lives in Tyler."

"You still carrying the torch?"

She bristled visibly, and her answer was emphatic. "No."

"Good," he drawled with a grin.

"Not that that's any of your business, either."

Porter spread his hands. "Just trying to make friendly conversation."

"Look, Mr. Wyman—"

"Hell, what's this mister baloney? You know my name. Use it."

"All right, Porter. What I was about to say— *again*—is that I'm not interested in dating."

He grinned. "Dating. Ah, now there's a word I didn't know was used anymore."

"Call it whatever you like."

"All I'm interested in is seeing you again."

"I've already told you—"

"I know, but let's just say I'm hard of hearing."

Ellen shook her head and smiled, though he could

tell it was unplanned. He sensed she would rather have glared at him. "I'm not going to argue with you."

"Good," he said again.

She sighed. "Look, it's been a long day, and I'm dead on my feet."

"I'm ready to go when you are."

Once they were in the truck and on the way back to the shop and her car, conversation was nonexistent. He wanted to push her to see him again, but he sensed he would run up against that same brick wall he'd run into in the restaurant. Still, he also sensed that she wasn't as immune to him as she wanted him to believe.

He'd caught her looking at him several times, and there was something in those eyes that he couldn't identify. Yet she was sitting rigidly beside him, staring straight ahead, while her perfume surrounded him, teasing him unmercifully.

Dammit, it wasn't fair.

"Thanks for dinner," she said, facing him after he'd pulled up next to her car and shoved the transmission into Park. She had her hand on the door handle.

"Hold on," he said. "I'll get the door."

She ran her tongue along her moist bottom lip. "That's not necessary."

What he did next wasn't necessary, either, but under no circumstances could he have stopped himself. He reached across the seat, latched onto her forearms and hauled her against his chest.

Her lips parted in a startled gasp. When they did,

he sank his into them. At first she remained lax, as if too stunned to react. But when he flicked his tongue against hers, she grabbed his shoulders and clung.

He increased the pressure, concentrating on her full bottom lip, sucking it between his teeth. She groaned, and for a moment she gave back as good as she was getting.

Then it was over. Both regained their senses at the same time and parted, breathing more heavily than if they had just run a marathon.

"Ellen, Ellen—" Porter broke off, having no idea what to say. Hell, there was nothing to say. He wasn't about to apologize for doing something he'd wanted to do since he'd laid eyes on her.

"Don't touch me again," she warned, her eyes flashing.

"I'd like to know why not. You enjoyed that kiss as much as I did."

"The hell I did."

He opened his mouth to respond, but he didn't get the chance. She opened the door to the truck and started to slide out.

"Dammit, Ellen, this is not going to end here."

"Oh, yes, it is."

"Why?"

"Because I'm not looking for a husband, that's why!"

"Who said I'm looking for a wife?"

"I'm not looking for someone to shack up with, either."

He opened his mouth to say he wasn't, either, but the words jammed in his throat.

"Gotcha!"

Before he could find a suitable comeback, she was out of the truck and inside her car.

Porter cursed as she drove away.

Eight

Ellen glanced in the mirror to make sure her head was still in place. Then, scoffing at such silliness, she turned and flounced into the bathroom where a tub of hot, scented water waited for her.

Every bone in her body ached from fatigue, but her mind was just the opposite. It felt as if it had been plugged into a live socket. Porter's kiss had nearly taken the top of her head off.

"Way to go, Ellen," she muttered under her breath, rubbing her forehead as if to make Porter's face and what had happened between them disappear.

She didn't know why she was acting like a virgin over the incident. A virgin she was not; an adult she was. So why wasn't she behaving like one? She had no clue. She also had no clue why this rough cowboy affected her as strongly as he did.

When he'd ground his lips into hers and their tongues had meshed, she hadn't wanted it to stop there. Dear Lord, she'd wanted more. With her face flaming, Ellen crossed to the tub and nearly dove in.

However, relaxing in that scented water was not a cure-all, not tonight, anyway. She felt as though a lit stick of dynamite had exploded inside her body. Maybe if she'd reacted to Samuel that way, their marriage wouldn't have gone down the tubes.

No, that hadn't been their problem, even though sex between them wasn't all that great. "Mundane" and "methodical" were the words that came to mind. Not wanting to think about Samuel and the past, Ellen washed her body with haste, got out, then dried off. When she strolled back into the bedroom, the bed beckoned. But she feared sleep wouldn't come. Her jumping-bean mind still held her weakened body captive.

She was right. Instead of sleeping, she kept thinking about Porter Wyman, and not just how his lips had made her wet, but how it would feel if he hadn't stopped with kissing her. In that twilight zone, she imagined his hands on her breasts, tugging her nipples into budding hardness. It was when he had a hand between her legs and a finger inside her panties that she lurched up in the bed, sweating.

Heavens! She was a mess, and just because of a kiss. Of course, she hadn't been kissed since her divorce, but that didn't make a whit of difference. It wasn't just the kiss she was fixated on, but rather the man who had kissed her.

Porter Wyman was not a man she would ever consider getting serious about, even if she were ready to take that step. He was too…rough for her.

The thought of him entering a theater and enjoying a play brought a smile to her lips. He would be as out of place there as she would be atop a horse. God forbid!

After concluding that if she wanted to get any sleep at all, she'd have to take something to knock her out. Those erotic images had left her feeling sick to her stomach.

Tomorrow would be a better day, she told herself as she swallowed two aspirins. She had made it clear to him that she was off limits. Nothing like that kiss would ever happen again. In fact, she doubted she would ever see him again.

But the Porter Wymans of the world didn't take rejection well. With that troubling thought haunting her, Ellen trotted back to the bed, climbed between the sheets and squeezed her eyes shut.

And prayed.

The smell of coffee scented the air, which meant business was booming. Ellen hadn't stopped all morning, but neither had Janis, who didn't have class, since it was Saturday.

Ellen wasn't complaining. She loved every minute of the hustle and bustle. Not only did it mean money in the coffer, but it brought her joy, gave her a feeling of accomplishment. Too, it proved that she had indeed made the right decision when she'd opened the shop in an area everyone said wouldn't work.

Ha!

She was having the last laugh and patting herself on the back. The only blight on her pleasure was a niggling fear that she would look up and see Porter stroll through the door.

Of course, gourmet coffee wasn't his thing any more than the theater would be. Not only that, it had been a week since he'd taken her to dinner and kissed her. It appeared her warning had made the impact she'd intended. Good, she told herself. She was happy with her life as it was.

"Ellen, phone," Janis said as she passed by with a tray of steaming mugs.

"Thanks. I'll take it in my office."

It was Meg.

"Hey, sis, what's up?"

"Nothing, really. Just wanted to say hi."

"How come I haven't seen you all week?" Ellen asked.

"Ralph's been home, and Kyle's been grounded. Need I say more?"

"I wish there had been another way," Ellen said, feeling awful because of her part in that fiasco.

"Me, too."

"How's he taking it?"

Meg sighed. "Driving me nuts."

"When's captivity over?"

"Today. He has a date with Miss Prissy tonight."

"Look, everything's going to be all right."

"Maybe. I wish I could tape a condom on *him* and pop a birth control pill into *her* mouth."

"Why, Megan Drysdale, the very idea! I'm shocked."

"No, you're not."

Ellen giggled. "You're right, I'm not. Actually I agree with you wholeheartedly."

"Kids!"

"I know, and I wish I had more time to talk, but we're swamped. Sure you don't want to come down and help?"

"I'd love to. But I can't. Ralph's not feeling good."

"Give him my best."

"I will." Meg paused. "By the way, have you talked to Porter lately?"

Ellen's heart almost stopped beating. "No, why?"

For reasons she thought were obvious, she hadn't confided in her sister about her date or the fact that Porter had kissed her. First Meg would chortle, then say I told you so, neither of which Ellen wanted to hear.

"He stopped by and talked to Ralph about possibly getting off the road and going to work locally."

"Really?"

"Really."

"Was that offer out of the blue, or had they talked before?"

"Out of the blue, actually."

"That's interesting."

"I thought so myself. You didn't say anything to him about our problems, did you?"

"You know better than that, Meggy."

"Sorry. I'm not thinking straight."

"Actually I didn't realize y'all were such good friends."

"We are and we aren't. Porter and Ralph go back a long way. Ralph used to hang around the equipment store, drinking coffee and such."

"So what did Ralph tell him?"

"Only that he'd think about it, but he won't. He's got the highway in his blood."

"Well, the doctor might have other ideas."

Meg sighed again. "Only time will tell. Look, I gotta run, and I know you do, too."

"You're right. Janis is probably in a tailspin."

Meg's sigh turned into a full-fledged groan. "Don't even mention her name."

Ellen felt the same about Porter, though she didn't voice that. She wished her sister hadn't mentioned *his* name.

"Keep the faith, sis."

"Maybe in another lifetime."

Ellen chuckled as she put down the receiver and walked out of her tiny cubbyhole, thanking her lucky stars once again that she didn't have a teenager. She would be pulling her hair out for sure.

When she walked back into the front, the tables were empty. Glancing at her watch, she noticed that it was closing time. Where had the day gone?

"I just about have everything cleaned up," Janis said, swinging a dishcloth in her hand.

"Then take off. I'll finish and lock up."

Thirty minutes later, she was about to do just that when she looked up and saw her landlord at the door. She wasn't pleased, but she didn't show it. Abe Fleming was a nice enough man, yet there was something about him that rubbed her the wrong way. Maybe it was the combination of his pompous attitude and plastic hair.

She hid a smile at the thought and motioned for him to come in.

"Didn't mean to wait till closing time," he said in his booming voice.

"No problem. Want a cup of coffee?"

"Don't mind if I do." He perched on a stool at the counter. "Iced cappuccino, if you don't mind. It's already hotter than hades out there."

"I know, and we're barely into summer." Ellen handed him a cup and watched as he took several sips, then licked his fat bottom lip. She turned away, wishing he'd drink up and leave.

"Do you have a minute?" he asked.

"Of course. What's up?"

Abe cleared his throat and shifted his eyes. "Man, this is good."

"Abe!"

He brought his gaze back to her. "Uh, I hate to tell you this—" He paused again.

Ellen held her breath. Something was up, something she knew she wasn't going to like. "Tell me what?" she persisted in a tight voice.

"I'm selling the building."

Her eyes widened. "Why?"

"Money, honey."

Ellen flinched at the "honey" while suddenly wishing he'd strangled on that coffee. "So what's the bottom line here?" She knew that, too, but she had to ask.

"You'll probably have to vacate the building."

"I'll be damned if I will."

Abe drew back, *his* eyes widening. "Whoa, little lady—"

"First off, I'm not your honey, and I'm not your little lady. Is that clear?"

"Er, right."

"Is it a done deal?"

"Almost, or will be next week."

"Do you know the new owner's plans for the building?"

Abe placed his hand on his hair; not one strand moved. Concentrating on something so insignificant seemed to be the glue that held her together. His announcement had been a kick in the stomach, and she was still reeling. The ramifications didn't bear thinking about, but she had no choice.

"Dunno. He didn't tell me. He just offered me a sum I couldn't pass up."

"I have a six month lease."

"You sure do." Abe drained his cup, then slid off the stool. "Whether or not he's open to renewing it is up to him. When the paperwork's final, I'm sure he'll be around."

"I'm sure he will—and boot me out."

"Sorry about that."

"Yeah, right."

When the door closed behind him, Ellen took deep breaths, but nothing could stop the tears. She raced into her office and grabbed a tissue.

"Daddy has to go."

Matthew's face screwed up, which meant trouble.

"I'll be back before you know it," Porter said in his most cajoling tone as he gazed at Bonnie, who stood ready to take his son from him.

They were outside, standing next to his truck. He should already have gone to the store, but he and his foreman had had things to do around the place. For some reason, the fish were dying in the large pond.

Although George had probably already shut down for the day, Porter nonetheless needed to go in and do some paperwork.

"Dada," Matthew was saying, reaching for him.

Porter tousled his son's nearly bald head. "You be a good boy for Bonnie, okay?"

Apparently it wasn't okay. Matthew started squalling.

"Don't worry," Bonnie said, holding the baby in her arms. "Once you're out of sight, he'll be fine."

Porter's face was grim. "I know. It's just that I hate to leave him crying."

"Go on. I'll take him for a wagon ride."

Porter climbed into the truck. "Later, then."

The housekeeper nodded, and he drove off. But he wasn't happy. Guilt had his stomach in a knot. He would never get used to leaving his son, even though he didn't have a choice. Dammit, Matt needed a mother, just not Wanda.

Instead of the road ahead, Ellen's face appeared before his eyes. His knuckles tightened around the steering wheel. "Damn!"

She was the last person he should be thinking about. She had no use for men or children. Yet he couldn't get the feel of her out of his system. He was horny, all right, as horny as hell. But he wanted Ellen Saxton, the one woman he couldn't have.

Why not? he asked himself. They were both free and over twenty-one. All he had to do was break down that prissy shield she'd erected and he would be home free.

Forget it, Wyman. She didn't want anything to do with him. But he didn't regret kissing her. If he had it to do over again, he'd repeat that kiss. She'd tasted so damn good, he hadn't wanted to let her go.

Still didn't.

Without realizing his intentions, he steered the truck in the opposite direction from the store. He might be making another mistake, but he would chance it. His gut instinct was urging him on. He'd learned long ago not to ignore that.

When he arrived at the coffee shop, the Closed sign was on the door, but it was unlocked. The hair stood up on the back of his neck.

"Ellen," he called, walking cautiously inside.

That was when he heard the muffled sound coming from the back room. Closing the door behind him, he moved across the room, his heart pounding in his throat.

"Ellen?" he called again.

She stepped out of the back room, her face drenched with tears. For a long moment they stared at each other. Finally, when fear let go of his throat, he asked, "What happened? Did someone hurt you?"

Nine

"See, I told you what you needed was some fresh air."

Ellen cut a glance at Porter, whose large but slender hands were wrapped around the truck's steering wheel. What she needed was a brain transplant for allowing herself to step out the door with him.

She didn't say that. The fault for her continued stupidity where Porter was concerned didn't lie with him. It rested on her shoulders. But he'd been so convincing once he'd found out that nothing terrible had happened to her.

When he'd demanded to know if someone had hurt her, she could have sworn she heard a tinge of panic, along with something else she couldn't identify, in his voice. Later, however, she told herself she'd been wrong. Like most men, he just didn't like to see a woman cry.

She had refused to tell him that she was being booted out of the building, a fact she still hadn't come to grips with. He'd continued to question her. "You weren't robbed, were you? Or worse?"

"Of course not," she'd snapped in an irritated voice.

His features cleared. "Okay, so you've had a bad day."

"You might say that."

His lips stretched into a full-blown smile. "Well, at least it started before you saw me. But I've made it worse, haven't I, waltzing in here unannounced?"

She would hardly call his gait a waltz, but she knew he was trying to make her feel better, joking, hoping to restore her good humor. She wasn't having any part of it. Seeing him made her want to pitch herself into his arms, to feel their strength surround her.

When she didn't answer, he went on, "Sure you don't want a shoulder to cry on?"

"I'll pass."

"So what *do* you want?"

Before she could answer, he held up his hands. "Don't answer that. I know. You want me to get lost."

Ellen bit down on her lower lip. "Honestly, I don't know what I want."

"Then let me make that decision for you."

"Why should I do that?"

"Because I have the guaranteed cure for making whatever ails you all better."

Ellen couldn't help but smile. "Is that a fact?"

"That's a hard fact," he drawled, shoving his hat back and grinning.

Not only could this man's kiss take the top of her head off, but his smile could charm the birds right out of the trees, as the old saying went. As usual, he was dressed in a casual shirt, jeans and boots. She wondered if he even owned a pair of dress pants or a suit. The thought of Porter in a suit almost made her laugh, though she knew he would be a knockout dressed in one. But she couldn't see that happening.

"Are you interested?"

Ellen tried to gather her scattered wits. "In what?"

"My cure."

She heard the hint of impatience in his tone, but she didn't care. "What is it?

"Come on, you'll see."

Her logical mind told her not to budge, but her troubled heart said to hell with logic. She'd grabbed her purse and locked the door behind them.

Now, riding through the wooded countryside, Ellen decided maybe Porter was right. This outing might indeed be the panacea she needed in order to cope with the bombshell her landlord had dropped in her lap.

"It is lovely, I'll admit, especially the wildflowers," she said, desperate not to think about her dilemma.

"You ain't seen nothing yet."

"Where are we going?"

"I was wondering when you'd ask that."

Ellen felt color rush into her face under his quick, hot gaze. "Well?" she said, hearing the breathlessness in her voice and hating it.

"My place."

"Oh, I don't think that's a good idea."

"It's a great idea, actually."

Ellen tried to control the panic building inside her. To go for a ride was one thing—harmless enough— but to go to his home was another matter. She had no intention of being that up close and personal.

"Do you always get your way?" Ellen squelched the urge to slug him verbally. He was so damn arrogant and self-assured, but at the same time so vulnerable. That combination drove her insane.

It was that kiss; that was the culprit. It seemed to dangle between them, tempting yet forbidden. If he dared to try to pull another stunt like that... Ellen nipped that thought in the bud before her expression gave her away.

"Maybe you'd feel better if you told me what had you in such a snit."

"It's none of your business," she snapped again.

"Ouch! That's twice you've bitten me."

"Then maybe you've learned your lesson."

He laughed. "Truce?"

"Depends."

"On what?"

"You taking me back to town."

"Not on your life."

"Porter, I—"

"Give it a rest. I'm not going to do anything you don't want me to."

Hearing the huskiness in his voice, Ellen knew he was referring to that kiss. Her stomach flip-flopped.

"Why am I not reassured?"

He chuckled. "Beats me."

Her silence apparently gave him the blessing he needed to increase the vehicle's speed. Soon they turned off the highway onto a road that most people would have missed. Sitting up a bit straighter, Ellen caught her breath. At the end of the road was a hill. On top of that hill was a sprawling ranch style home.

She faced him, her eyes wide. "Is that yours?"

"Yep. You like?"

"It's...beautiful." She didn't know why she was so surprised. After all, Meg had said he had more money than most people have sense. But somehow, this man and this house didn't go together.

"Thanks, but then I'm rather partial. I built it myself."

She flashed him an incredulous look. "You're kidding?"

"Nope. Oh, I had to subcontract some of it, but for the most part, these beat-up hands hammered every nail," he said as he pulled to a stop in front of the house.

"A man of many talents."

He didn't reply to that. He didn't have to. The smoldering look he gave her before he climbed out of the truck brought another flush to her cheeks.

What had she gotten herself into? In *her* vulnerable state, he was a danger to both her mind and body.

For the time being, she was here, so she might as well make the best of it, though she had no idea what she was about to encounter.

She dared not look at him for fear of seeing that taunting grin on his face. "Is Matthew here?" she asked, scrambling out of the cab before he could extend a helping hand. It wouldn't do for him to touch her.

"He's around somewhere. No telling what he and Bonnie are up to."

"Bonnie?"

"You know. The housekeeper/nanny."

"Ah, yes, the jewel."

He gave her an odd look, but he didn't say anything.

On the inside, the house was homey and not the least bit ostentatious. Yet there was something about it that said a man hadn't decorated it. Either his ex-wife or an interior designer had been at work.

"Bonnie!" Porter called, closing the front door behind him.

"In here."

He gestured to show the way. "They're in the kitchen."

Their whereabouts were obvious as the smell of homemade bread permeated the air. Ellen placed her hand across her stomach before it growled. Her movement didn't go unnoticed.

"Me, too," Porter said with a grin, then pointed to his left.

The housekeeper had her back to the open door and was standing in front of the cabinet. The baby was in a high chair close by. When Matthew saw his daddy, he squealed and clapped his little hands.

"You're just in time for some hot bread," Bonnie said, swinging around with a smile on her face, only to have it completely disappear when she saw that Porter wasn't alone.

"Oops, sorry, didn't know you'd brought company," she added in a low tone, her gaze landing on Ellen and remaining there, her eyebrows raised.

"Bonnie Temple, Ellen Saxton," Porter said as he strode toward his son and lifted him out of the chair. "Ellen owns the new coffee shop in town."

"Nice to meet you," Ellen said.

"Same here," the housekeeper responded, then seemed uncertain what to say or do next.

Ellen sensed instantly that Bonnie was anything *but* pleased to meet her. Jealousy was the reason that came to mind. Apparently Porter didn't bring many women around the place. Mmm, now that was interesting. Maybe he had something going with Bonnie. Despite the fact that she was older, she was attractive. Not liking the way her thoughts were heading, Ellen switched them back to the moment at hand.

"I'm going to show Ellen around," Porter said to Bonnie. "We'll push Matthew in the stroller."

"Don't you want some hot bread first?"

Porter turned to Ellen, a question in his eyes.

"No, I'm fine," Ellen said hastily, grinning at Matthew, who was grinning back.

"Catch you later, then," Porter said.

In a few minutes, the three of them were outside,

walking the path through the woods. Matthew was laughing and pointing at everything.

"He seems such a happy and contented baby," Ellen commented, enjoying this outing more than she was willing to admit.

"He is, which is a damn miracle, considering what he's been through." The unvarnished bitterness was there in his tone.

"It's hard to believe his mother just took off. How could she leave him?"

"Beats the hell out of me."

Ellen didn't respond.

"But I'm glad she did. We don't need her."

"I can understand why. Bonnie appears to be doing a marvelous job."

"I told you, I couldn't do without her."

That statement smarted, which made Ellen furious. She didn't have any claims on this man, for God's sake. So what was her problem? As far as she was concerned, he and Bonnie could make whoopee every night.

"She's just my housekeeper."

Ellen raised startled eyes to his. "I didn't say—"

"You didn't have to. I saw those wheels turning in your head."

"Damn you," she muttered.

He merely laughed, which made her feel more like a fool than ever. To overcome her embarrassment, Ellen leaned over, pulled Matt's stroller closer to her and tickled him on the chin.

They had stopped by a creek in the woods, where two cement benches faced one another. The baby kicked, laughed and flailed his hands. When she looked up, Porter was watching her. Their eyes locked.

Ellen almost reeled visibly against the jolt of electricity that seemed to zap her body. Yet she couldn't remove her gaze.

"You should have a child of your own, you know."

She jerked her eyes away. "Motherhood's not for me."

"I disagree. I think you'd make a swell mother."

"That's because you don't know me."

"I'd like to change that."

Again her eyes met his. "Porter—"

"Okay, I won't push, for now."

She rubbed her right temple. "Look, I'm just not ready for another relationship."

"Me, either."

"Then—"

"Taking you to dinner and showing you my place isn't my definition of a relationship."

"What about kissing me?" she blurted before she thought.

He removed his Stetson, while his eyes pierced hers. "Well, I reckon that could figure into the definition."

"You're impossible."

"So what do you say?"

"About what?"

"Seeing me again."

Ellen hesitated. "Don't push it."

"It's your call." He didn't say anything for a long

moment. When he did, he changed the subject. "I still want to know what upset you at the store. I hate like the dickens to see a woman cry."

"It's really nothing."

"You're not the type to cry over nothing."

"You'll hound me till I tell you, won't you?"

"You're a quick learner," Porter said, grinning.

Ellen told him about her landlord's stunt. When she finished, he cursed a blue streak.

Her gaze turned to Matthew. "You'd best watch your mouth. Your son's taking in every word you say." Her tone was teasing, though she was secretly pleased that he was concerned about her plight.

"What are you going to do?"

"I haven't the foggiest."

"Want me to get a piece of that bastard?"

"Absolutely not. You stay out of it."

"Yes, ma'am."

Ellen glared at him. "I mean—"

The rest of the warning never got past her lips. He stopped it with *his* lips. They latched onto hers with a vengeance—hot and long-lasting—at the same time that a hand found her breast and squeezed it.

She never knew which was the loudest—her heart or the sound of Matthew's gleeful laughter as he watched them. And she didn't care.

Drinking the moisture from his mouth and having his hand on her body was all that mattered.

Ten

Porter leaned back in his chair in the store's office and crossed his hands behind his head. Staring at the ceiling solved nothing, nor did wallowing in his stupidity.

With that thought, he lunged up and strode into the store proper. Silence greeted him. Today was Sunday, and it was closed and would remain that way all day. Standing there, Porter felt his good judgment return, and a calmness stole over him.

Things weren't as bad as they seemed, right?

Yes, they were, he quickly amended. He was smitten with a woman who didn't give a damn if she ever saw him again. Since Wanda had walked out on him, he was used to being chased, *not* doing the chasing.

Porter almost smiled at that thought, but he didn't. Smiles, usually his trademark and easy to come by, were in short supply of late, thanks to a lady named Ellen. He eyed a shiny new red tractor, the latest and most updated model he had on his showroom floor. That was what he ought to be concentrating on. He had taken a twin of that machine home with him, and he'd been itching to get on it and mow the south pasture.

Unfortunately that itch had been replaced by another one—a baser itch. Kissing Ellen again had sent his life spinning in another direction, one that he wasn't ready for but wanted anyway.

Lust.

That was what motivated him, and he knew it. But he didn't know what to do about it, especially when Ellen apparently didn't return that particular sentiment. She'd kissed him back, all right, but she hadn't wanted to. When they had broken apart, both as limp as if they had just made love, she had been pasty white.

"If you expect me to say I'm sorry this time, I'm—"

She'd held up her hand, stalling his words. "It's obvious I can't expect anything from you, that I can't trust you."

"Explain that," he retorted, taking umbrage to that statement.

"That's not necessary. You know how I felt—" This time Ellen's words dried up, and she turned away, but not before he saw her flushed face, a flush he knew wasn't caused by the weather.

"You kissed me back." His tone was harder and more accusing than he'd intended. But dammit, he was frustrated. The bulge behind his jeans was hammer-hard, which was uncomfortable as hell, something he wasn't used to.

Ellen didn't say anything. She simply jutted her chin.

"Look, we're both adults here, right?"

"I think we've been down this road before."

Clamping down on his mounting frustration, Porter softened his tone, even though the words still made their point. "So you want me, and I want you. What's wrong with that?"

Ellen slid her eyes toward him. "I told you, I'm not ready to get involved with anyone."

"Me, either."

"So you just want to have sex with me?"

This time *his* face flushed. "Yes, dammit, I do, and I think you want that, too."

"Sex for the sake of sex is not my thing."

"Mine, either."

"If that's the case, then we should back off now."

Porter blew out a breath and forced himself to lighten up. That creep she'd been married to must have done a number on her. He would just have to curb his own lust and be patient, or he'd drive her away for sure.

"I don't want to stop seeing you."

She looked out across the pasture. "Let's just take it easy and see what happens."

"Is it Matt?"

She turned back to him and didn't hesitate, for which he was glad. "Partly."

He blanched, but at least she was honest. He

couldn't take underhanded women. Wanda had the habit of saying one thing and meaning another.

"That's not to say he's not darling," she added quickly, "because he is. It's just that—"

"I know. You don't have to draw me a picture. Like you said earlier, you're not into motherhood."

"Look, right now I don't really know what I'm into. I have a lot on my mind, mainly what I'm going to do about the shop."

"Fine. I'll give you some space. But I'm not backing off." Porter paused then grinned. "I want you, Ellen Saxton, and I won't give up."

She sighed, but she couldn't keep from grinning as she did. "You're one stubborn man. But for now, would you please take me home?"

"You bet." He tipped his hat, though what he wanted instead was to haul her back in his arms and finish what he'd started, thinking how it would feel to run his hands *under* her bra, finger her nipples until they were as hard as he was. Instead he forced his thoughts back to the harsh reality and escorted her to the truck.

That conversation had taken place yesterday.

Now, here he was thinking about her again, aching to see her. Well, he couldn't. What he could do was take his son fishing. Being with Matthew always put things in perspective. When he decided to get serious about a woman, which meant more than getting inside her pants, it would be someone who loved children, who actually wanted one of her own.

He wanted to make love to Ellen Saxton, *not* marry her. Therein lay the problem. Until he felt her naked, scented skin next to his, he wouldn't be able to let her go.

Not wanting to think about her anymore, he locked up and got into his truck. An off-the-wall idea struck him, and instead of heading home, he headed in the opposite direction.

He knew he was about to meddle where he shouldn't. It wouldn't be the first time, and it sure as hell wouldn't be the last.

Porter pressed down on the gas pedal.

"I'm for taking a contract out on him," Meg said grimly.

Ellen actually smiled, though Meg couldn't see it. They were visiting on the phone. "Works for me. Know anyone in that line of business?"

"Mmm, let me see. We might have to go to Houston."

"You're terrible. But you know that, don't you?"

"What I am is someone who doesn't like to see the people she cares about get rooked."

"It's my own fault."

"That's a crock."

"If I'd signed the lease for longer, the snake wouldn't have a leg to stand on. But I was afraid the shop wouldn't fly."

"That's partly my fault," Meg said, sounding down-in-the-mouth. "I wasn't exactly all that encouraging."

"Yes, you were."

"I just wanted you here, in 'Doches. I wasn't too worried about your business."

"Don't blame yourself, for heaven's sake. What I did was my decision, and I accept full responsibility."

"So what are you going to do?"

"Pray that the new owner lets me stay. Meanwhile, I'm going to go out and look for a place to move to just in case."

"God, what a nightmare."

"Nightmare or not, I have to do it."

"I'll go with you."

"I'll holler if I need you. Right now, you've got enough on your own plate. By the way, how are things on the old homefront?"

"Kyle's as obnoxious as ever, but I adore him." Ellen chuckled.

"And Ralph's back on the road, though I don't know how long that's going to last."

"My offer still stands if you need—"

"Don't. I'm not taking any money from you."

"Okay, okay," Ellen said. "Don't get bent out of shape."

"Why don't you come over?"

"Thanks, but I'm going to hang around the house today and water my plants and wash clothes."

"All those have-to things. We'll talk later." Meg paused. "Try not to worry about the shop. Something will work out. I know it will."

"I hope you're right. While I can always return to Tyler, I don't want to."

"Them words are music to my ears, sis."

Ellen laughed as she hung up the receiver, only to hear the doorbell ring almost immediately. Who on earth? she asked herself, frowning. She looked like something the cat dragged in, dressed in denim shorts and a T-shirt. On top of that, she was barefoot.

When she reached the door and checked her peephole, her jaw dropped, followed by the racing of her heart. Porter. What was he doing standing on her porch?

"Ellen?"

"What?"

"Can I come in?"

"Dammit, Porter—"

"Please."

His tone didn't beg, but there was a certain something in it that she couldn't identify. And it was that "something" that got him what he wanted. She unlatched the door and opened it. But that was as far as this would go. He wasn't about to get past her. What he had to say would be said there, on the porch.

"Aren't you going to invite me in?"

"No."

He grinned. "I've never seen your house."

"You'll live."

An eyebrow shot up. "Which is another way of saying 'get lost.'"

The corners of Ellen's mouth quivered as she leaned against the door for support. Why did he always have to look and smell so good? He looked as though he'd just gotten out of the shower, though she doubted that was true, not in midafternoon.

The moisture she saw glistening on the hairs at his neck was probably sweat. Even that turned her on. She suddenly wondered how that sweat would taste if she were to place her tongue on that spot and lick.

Swallowing a moan, Ellen clung more tightly to the door. How could she be thinking such things? She'd never thought about doing something like that to her ex.

What made this cowboy so different, so attractive to her?

Porter wasn't the type of man she should be interested in. If she'd met him in Tyler, she wouldn't have given him the time of day. Or would she?

He had a certain sexual charisma that cut to the core. And when he'd fondled her breasts, she hadn't wanted him to stop, which was exactly why she couldn't let him inside. Not only didn't she trust him, but she also didn't trust herself.

She wasn't about to get involved in a torrid affair. That was not what she was about. When she made love to a man, she wanted it to mean something.

"What are you thinking about?" Porter asked, his tone as husky as his eyes were lazy.

"Nothing," she lied, praying that he hadn't read her mind.

"Probably the same thing I was," he added, as if she hadn't spoken.

"What do you want?" she demanded, forcing a coolness into her tone.

"Your time."

"Porter!"

"I know we agreed to give each other space, but it's such a beautiful day, and I thought—"

"You thought what?" she interrupted impatiently.

"That you might like to go fishing."

She didn't know what she'd expected him to say,

but it wasn't that. Her mouth flopped open, then she recovered and said, "Fishing? You've got to be kidding."

"I don't kid about that."

"Well, I don't fish."

"Sure you do. You just don't know it yet."

Eleven

The day was sunny and perfect. The pasture was serene and lovely. The pond was cool and calm. The boat was new and shiny. Still, Ellen wished she were anywhere but here, in this boat in the middle of the huge pond.

"Having fun yet?" Porter asked, humor coloring his voice as he whipped his casting rod back, then forward. She watched as the ugly plastic critter on the other end plopped into the water.

"Not yet."

"It's because you're not trying."

Ellen cut him a sharp glance, then said in a prim tone, "Remember, this is your thing, not mine."

Porter's eyes sparkled, and his lips broke into a ready smile. "Sitting with your legs crossed and your back rigid, you look like a teacher who just bit into an apple that her worst student gave her.'' He paused. ''You interested in the rest of that story?''

''Not really,'' she responded, her tone coated with good-natured sarcasm.

''That apple was worm infested.''

''Funny.''

''Ah, come on, be a sport.''

''That's easy for you to say.'' Ellen wrinkled her nose as she peered into the bucket next to Porter's right ankle. It was filled with live worms for baiting her cane pole. Watching them crawl around in the container, she shuddered.

Porter was watching her, an amused expression rearranging his features. He was loving every minute of torturing her. But then, she had no one but herself to blame. When he'd mentioned the word fishing, she should have said no way, then slammed the door in his face.

Obviously she hadn't. And he had charmed her into his outing. Now she should give her uptightness a rest and make the best of the situation. After all, it wouldn't last much longer, and she certainly wasn't in any danger.

''Sure you don't want to try your hand at catching a white perch?'' He was smiling.

Ellen glared at him. ''Not hardly. I'm content to watch you pull 'em in.''

''You sure?''

''Believe me, I'm sure.''

He grinned, then turned his back and cast again, allowing her the privilege of watching his athletic body perform in all its glory. His shoulders were strong, and his biceps bulged every time he wielded the rod.

The pleasure didn't end there. His waist tapered into a tush that was about as perfect as she'd ever seen, not that she made a habit of studying men's rears. Yet a woman would have to be blind not to notice Porter's.

Suddenly Ellen wondered what it would feel like to run her fingers over... Stop it! she told herself, switching her gaze and taking a deep, gulping breath. She had never reacted to a man with such wanton lust. In fact, Samuel had often accused her of being frigid.

She had begun to think that maybe she was. Now she knew better. This cowboy had only to look at her with his smoldering gaze to make her ache with desire. However, she had no intention of assuaging that ache.

Sex for the sake of sex was no good. And neither was motherhood, unless you were ready for it.

"What are you thinking about?"

Porter's husky voice jerked her out of her wool-gathering. "Nothing important."

"Are you getting tired?"

"Not really."

"Bored?"

Ellen peered up at him. Even though the sun was in her eyes, she could see the humor that marked the lines in his face. "What would you say if I said yes?"

"I'd say I'm not surprised."

"That doesn't make you mad?"

"Why should it? You're here, regardless."

"You're right about that." She paused. "Does anything ever rile you?"

"Yeah, lots."

"Care to elaborate?"

"Stick around long enough and you'll find out." Porter's stare was guarded, but his words were loaded with unspoken meaning.

Ellen decided against responding to that comment as she had no intention of sticking around—at least, not around *him*.

"I hope to stay in 'Doches, if I don't have to close the shop."

"Oh, I don't think that's—" Unexpectedly his words were chopped off as his rod jerked so hard that for a second Ellen feared he might lose his balance.

"All right!" he muttered, reeling in the fish that was yanking on the end of the line. "I wish Matt could see this. He'd have a fit."

"You mean you take that baby out in this boat?"

"Why not? He loves it."

When they'd arrived at the ranch, Matthew had been asleep. She'd been strangely disappointed, as she'd wanted to see the little fellow. For some reason she seemed to like him more than most babies she'd been around. It wasn't because of Porter, either. Maybe she was more in tune with children than she'd thought.

But then, Matt was a special child. He was happy and well-adjusted, all the more reason to admire Porter, something she didn't really want to do. And let's not forget about Bonnie, she told herself. Where Matt was concerned, she deserved her share of the credit.

It was obvious to her, though apparently not to Porter, that Bonnie would like to take care of him with the same diligence she took care of his son. Maybe she was the right woman for Porter.

That thought was suddenly too distasteful for Ellen to think about.

"Come on, be a good boy and come on in," Porter whispered in a coaxing voice.

Thankful for the interruption, Ellen refocused her attention on Porter, realizing he was talking to the fish. She rolled her eyes toward the unblemished sky. Men and their misguided ideas of fun.

Nonetheless, she watched in awe, and not without admiration, as Porter grabbed the net and placed it under what looked to be the biggest fish she'd ever seen.

When he swung his catch over into the boat and the slimy thing began flopping all over the place, her admiration ended.

"Jeez Louise!" she hollered, jumping up and doing her best to dodge the floundering fish.

"Hey, be careful, you'll—"

Porter's warning came too late. When Ellen moved sharply sideways, the boat chose that moment to rock. She lost her balance.

"*Ohhh!*" she cried, feeling herself fall backward.

Porter's hand shot out, but his efforts proved too little too late.

"Ellen!"

His cry did nothing to stop her from hitting the water. She landed with a splash, then felt herself immediately sink toward the sandy bottom.

Panic seized her by the throat, and she squeezed her eyes shut, struggling to hold her breath under the cool darkness that surrounded her. Fight! she told herself, even as she used her arms and legs to claw and kick her way to the surface.

Finally she made it, only to find Porter in the water beside her, reaching for her.

"Can't you swim?"

"No," she managed to gasp.

He cursed, then said, "Hold on, I've got you."

She felt his arms around her upper body, and without knowing or caring how, she found herself back in the boat. Moments later she was wrapped in a huge towel and the boat was at the edge of the bank.

Silence hovered between them as they stared at each other. Ellen knew what she must look like—a drowned dog or worse.

"Why the hell didn't you tell me you couldn't swim?"

"Would it have made any difference?"

"Damn right. I would've insisted you wear a life jacket. I should have anyway. I don't know what the hell I was thinking."

He seemed to be mumbling more to himself than to her, which was just fine. She didn't want to hear anything he had to say, anyway. She wanted to go home and nurse her misery in private.

"Look, I'm sorry," he said.

"No, you're not."

"Dammit, I said I was sorry, and I meant it."

"Go ahead."

"And do what?" He sounded perplexed.

"Laugh. You're dying to."

"Damn. You're the most paranoid woman I've ever known."

His frustration was apparent even as he shoved a hand through his dripping hair. That was when she realized he was as wet as she was and didn't look a bit better. In fact, he looked worse than a drowned rat.

Suddenly laughter spilled past Ellen's lips. Later she suspected that laughter stemmed from hysteria and shock that, first, she'd even stepped into a boat, and second, that she'd fallen out of it.

"You…you look so—" She couldn't go on.

"I wouldn't say anything if I were you," Porter said, his eyes twinkling. "It's a toss-up as to who's the worse for wear. Although I'll have to admit, I didn't think I'd ever see you in this state."

"And whose fault is that?" Ellen lashed back, her eyes flashing.

"You're obviously hankering for a fight. But I'm not going to put my gloves on. The truth is, even though you took a dunking, you still look like you just walked off the fashion pages."

"Flattery won't work. Besides, I can't believe you're actually familiar with the fashion ads." Her words were syrupy.

"Watch your mouth, woman!"

Ellen pushed strands of hair out of her eyes at the same time that her mouth turned down. "What a mess. If my sister could only see me now."

"Knowing Meg, she'd love it."

"Underneath, you're loving every minute of this, too, aren't you?"

"If I say yes, you're going to get mad."

"Probably."

"Then mum's the word. Hell, I'm trying to get out of the doghouse, not back in it."

Ellen giggled, deciding she might as well laugh some more. Her only other alternative was to cry, and she wasn't in the mood to do that.

Her giggle triggered his laughter. Once they started, they couldn't seem to stop.

"Excuse me."

Their laughter stopped as abruptly as it had begun. They swung around. Bonnie stood behind them, her mouth twisted as if she'd been sucking on bitter weeds. Uh-oh, Ellen thought, picking up on her hostility instantly. However, she doubted Porter was aware of it, especially as he asked, "Where's Matt?"

"In his playpen, but he's unhappy."

"What do you mean, he's unhappy?"

"I can't get him to stop crying."

Porter's features registered concern. "Is he sick?"

"'Fretful' is a better word." Bonnie seemed to shutter her eyes before she added, "I, er, think he wants you."

So do you, Ellen thought waspishly.

"All right, Bonnie," Porter said in a vexed tone, "we'll be up shortly."

Silence filled the space until Bonnie was out of earshot, then Porter scratched his head and said, "I don't get it."

"Yes, you do. You just don't want to admit it."

"What's to admit?"

"You figure it out. Now, if you don't mind, I'd like to go home."

He gave her a strange look, then drawled, "Your wish is my command."

Meg took a gulp of her cappuccino, staring at Ellen over the rim.

"I wish I could've seen you."

"No, you don't. Trust me."

Meg shook her head. "I'd almost give my left boob, in fact."

"Megan Drysdale, you're awful. That's awful!"

"You're right, it is, and I was just kidding. Anyhow, Ralph wouldn't be too happy about that."

"How did we get off on that?" Ellen raised her hand. "Don't answer. I know. Your perverted sense of humor, that's how."

"You're right. But at least it's keeping us sane."

Ellen wasn't sure about the "us" part. She remained a basket case. She had left the shop with Janis and another part-time helper and, with Meg's help, had scouted the downtown area for other locations.

So far, they had come up empty-handed. Ellen was trying her best not to panic, but if something didn't turn up soon, she wouldn't have any choice.

Over coffee, however, they had opted not to discuss or dwell on the dilemma. Instead the conversation had turned to her outing with Porter.

"So did you have a good time?"

"Yeah, kind of," Ellen admitted reluctantly.

"'Kind of' my ass."

"Megan, watch your mouth!"

"Okay, but admit you enjoyed every minute you were with him, even the dip in the water."

"No way will I ever admit that."

"Why don't you just go ahead and sleep with him?" Megan ignored the gasp that erupted from Ellen's mouth and went on. "It's bound to happen, you know."

"I don't know any such thing and neither do you."

Megan raised her hands. "Sorry, didn't mean to get your blood pressure up."

"Yes, you did."

Meg smiled. "Maybe I did. I just want to keep you here. If Porter's the glue, then—"

"He isn't and won't ever be."

Janis appeared at the table, stifling the conversation.

"Mrs. Drysdale, you have a phone call."

After Megan had gone to her office to take the call, Ellen released a pent-up sigh. If only she could find a place to move her shop. If only that jerk Abe hadn't sold the building out from under her. According to the rumor mill, it was to be torn down.

Although she'd had no official word from Abe on that score, she didn't doubt the rumor.

"It's the school," Meg said, coming up to stand in front of her.

"Kyle?"

"Yep."

"What now?"

"He was in a fight."

"Oh no."

"I can think of something much stronger to say, but you wouldn't approve."

"Want me to come with you?"

"Nope. You've got enough to worry about. I'll call you."

Ellen got up and gave her sister a big hug. "Hang in there."

"You, too."

Once Meg was gone, Ellen took her unfinished coffee and went into her office. The shop wasn't busy, since it was midafternoon. Maybe she could get some much-needed book work done.

She was in the process of doing just that when she looked up and saw Porter standing in the doorway. Her heart lurched, as it always did when he came anywhere near.

"What are you doing here?" she demanded, not having seen him since the boating fiasco three days ago now.

"You don't have to worry about finding another location for your shop," he said without preamble.

"Why is that?"

"Because I took care of it."

Ellen leaned back in her chair and stared at him, her lips in a pencil-straight line. "What do you mean?"

"*I* bought the building."

Twelve

George scratched his head, then shook it. "You're asking me a question like that? Hell, man, I don't know nothing about women."

"Does anyone?" Porter muttered grimly.

He and George were in the office at the store. They had been going over orders for several big companies to make sure everything was on the right track. Porter hated foul-ups, both personal and in business.

Of late, his personal life had certainly been one big foul-up. If he hadn't had Matt to go home to, he didn't know what he would have done. For the kid, he'd marry that airhead Wanda all over again.

"What's going on?" George demanded, "If you don't mind me asking, that is."

"I thought I was doing someone a favor—" Porter broke off and blew a strong gust of air from his lungs.

"Go on. You've got my ear, even if it's sore." As if to make good on his words, George rubbed his swollen right ear.

Porter frowned. "What bit you?"

"Not no woman, that's for damn sure." George grinned.

Porter didn't return his smile.

"Sorry, didn't mean to make light of your trouble."

"It's not you," Porter said, a grim note in his voice. "It's me. I screwed up. Again."

"Tell me it doesn't have anything to do with your ex."

"God, no. At least, not for the moment, although she did call my attorney about Matt."

"So what's got you so bent out of shape?"

"It's personal."

George slid farther down in his chair. "I've got all the time in the world."

"I've been seeing this woman."

"Seeing as in—"

"Never mind." Porter cut in darkly.

George gave him a knowing look.

"Anyway, she owns the new coffee shop downtown. It's off and running, doing really well."

"So what's the problem?"

"The problem is, the landlord sold the building and told her the new owner would probably boot her out as soon as her lease was up."

"Ah, so that's where *your* favor comes in."

"Right. *I* bought the building."

"Damn, Porter, the last thing you need is something else to look after."

Porter leaned forward. "It's a good investment. I didn't know it was for sale or I would've snapped it up earlier."

"Sounds like you solved your friend's problem."

"I thought so, too."

"I don't get it."

"She's pissed."

"Who's pissed?"

"The lady who owns the coffee shop, the lady I mentioned seeing."

"That word 'seeing,' my friend, covers a large tract of real estate, but we'll let that pass for the time being. Why's she pissed?"

"That's what I'd like to know."

"What did she say?"

"She told me to unbuy it."

"Unbuy it? You're kiddin' me."

"Nope. She got madder than a hornet that's been sprayed with bug killer."

"Surely she gave you a reason for telling you to unbuy it, whatever the hell that means."

"Said she didn't want me or any man doing her any favors."

George's eyebrows elevated. "Sounds to me she don't like men. You sure she ain't one of those—"

"No, she's not gay, for heaven's sake. I told you, I'd been seeing her."

"Uh, right."

"Hell, I don't know why I said anything to you to start with."

George stood, then grinned. "Me, either. Don't worry about it, would be my advice. Hell, the next time you see her, she'll probably throw her arms around you and give you a big kiss of thanks. You know how woman change their minds."

"Yeah."

"Sorry I couldn't be more help."

Porter didn't respond. He hadn't expected George to come through with any sage advice. He guessed he'd just needed a sounding board. Why didn't he feel better?

"Well, I'd best get this moneymaker open," George said, his grin expanding. "And make more of it. You might need the money to buy another building."

Porter's glance was murderous. "Get outta here."

George shuffled out the door, his deep laughter filling the air.

Porter leaned back in his chair, the scowl on his features deepening. What to do? He didn't have a clue. He thought he'd pulled off a miracle. Instead he'd been slapped in the face—not physically, of course. That wasn't Ellen's style. She was too cool and calm for that, at least on the outside. Now inside...

He shifted in his chair, feeling himself grow hard in anticipation of finding out what really simmered underneath that cool facade. He would bet there was plenty of heat, and he would love nothing better than to light the match and set off the fireworks.

"In your dreams, Wyman," he mumbled under his breath.

After she'd stripped him of his hide when he'd told her about buying the building, he doubted she would let him within ten feet of her.

But then again, he'd never been a quitter. He didn't see any reason to start now.

"Are you sick?"

Heartsick, she wanted to say, but didn't. Instead she gave her sister, who stood at her door, a wan smile. "My tummy's a little queasy, that's all."

"Mmm, that's enough." Meg pushed past her. "I brought you some soup and other soothing goodies. I know you don't have anything fit to eat in your fridge."

"Sure you want to come in? What I have might be catching." Ellen knew better; she was just talking to hear her head rattle. Her nerves were the culprit here, and she knew it. Yet that was hard to admit, even to herself. At the moment, she preferred to be alone; that was why she'd left the shop and come home. But she could hardly tell her sister that.

"Thanks for taking care of me," Ellen said as Meg walked back into the living area.

"Anytime."

"Do you have time for a cup of tea?"

"No, actually, I don't. I have to be at the school for a meeting with Kyle's principal."

"What's the latest on that? Since you got that call at the shop, we haven't had time to talk."

"It's Kyle's smart mouth." Meg's face was troubled. "He used it on the wrong person, and he knocked Kyle for a loop. Of course, Kyle got right back up and belted him.''

"Oh, dear.''

"And wouldn't you know it, Ralph's on the road. And when he's here, he's no help. They just don't see eye to eye on anything. That's part of Kyle's problem.''

"Oh, Meggy, I wish there was something I could do to help.''

"You do. You listen to my bellyaching.''

"That's tit for tat. You listen to mine.''

"Speaking of yours, what's the latest on the building? Is the new landlord going to make you leave?''

Ellen's mouth stretched into a thin line. "There's been a new development there.''

"Oh no. From the look on your face, it's not good.''

"Porter Wyman's the new owner.'' Her tone was as dull as her eyes.

Meg gasped. "Excuse me?''

"You heard right.''

"Then you won't have to move after all.'' Megan's voice was thick with excitement.

"That's debatable.''

"Debatable? Are you nuts? You ought to be jumping through hoops, girl, instead of sitting there like you've just been diagnosed with a terminal illness.''

"It's not that simple, or at least it's not to me.''

"You *are* nuts.''

"I don't expect you to understand.''

"What's to understand, except you're looking a gift horse in the mouth.''

Ellen felt her stomach do another flip inside her. Meg must have picked up on that; her features and her tone of voice changed. They both softened. "Look, obviously there's something going on that I don't know about."

Tears gathered at the corners of Ellen's eyes, which added to her anger. "That kind of high-handedness is something Samuel would've done. It's my problem, and I would have solved it. Somehow."

"Oops, I didn't think about that."

"You weren't supposed to."

"Look, we'll talk about it some more later," Meg said. "Right now, you should go to bed. You're turning green around the gills. I'll call you later, okay?"

Ellen gave her a wan smile. "Thanks again. I promise we'll talk."

"That we will. Meanwhile, you let that sleeping dog lie."

"Meaning?"

"Don't you dare say anything that would make Porter change his mind."

"Megan! Didn't you hear anything I said? I *want* him to change his mind."

"No, you don't. Trust me on that."

Before Ellen could respond properly, Meg walked out and slammed the door behind her.

"Damn," Ellen whispered, then got up and made her way into the kitchen, where she made herself another cup of peppermint tea.

When she returned to the sofa and sat down, she scooted her feet under her. She had removed her clothes and slipped into a robe, thankful that she'd had enough sense to leave the shop early.

Business had been slow, and Janis and her other helper were now capable of handling things. And her stomach had been legitimately bothering her and still was, thanks to that stunt Porter had pulled and their subsequent verbal skirmish.

When he'd sauntered into her office and made his announcement, she'd been as shocked as she'd been angry.

"This is a joke, right?" she'd said, feeling her temper rise along with her temperature.

"Hardly, not when you're talking about that kind of money."

"Why would you do a thing like that?"

"Why not?"

"Dammit, Porter, I'm serious."

"Hey, what's the matter? I thought that was what you wanted."

"I didn't want to move. You're right about that."

"Then why are you looking at me like I'm a two-headed monster?"

"Because you overstepped your bounds."

"Ellen, you're not making sense."

"I'm making perfect sense. Stop the deal."

"Like hell I will."

She stood and glared at him. "I won't let you buy this building. Not for me, that is."

"Okay, so I bought it for me."

"You just don't get it, do you?"

"I sure as hell don't."

"I want you to leave."

He stared at her as if *she* was now the two-headed monster. "Leave? Just like that?"

"Yes."

A muscle jerked in his jaw. "Fine."

With that he spun on his booted feet and stomped out.

Now, two days later, she still hadn't come to grips with the incident or made peace with it. She doubted she ever would and consequently didn't know what to do.

Damn him for further complicating her life.

The doorbell pealed. Thinking it was Meg again, she knew she had to answer it, but she didn't want to. She was enjoying her time alone and didn't want company.

"Is that you, Meggy?"

When she didn't get an answer, she frowned but unbolted the door anyway.

Porter stood on the porch, hat in hand. When he saw her, he cocked his head and gave her a sheepish grin. "Can I come in?"

Thirteen

Ellen's first inclination was to say an emphatic no and tell him to go away. But she didn't. Later, she didn't know why, except he looked so endearing, so enticing, standing there with his hat in his hand, that she literally caved in.

Without speaking, she stepped aside, knowing that what she was doing was a dumb move. But she was too tired to argue with him anymore. More to the point, what would a belligerent attitude accomplish? If she was going to beat him at his own game, she had to keep her emotions under wraps.

It was while they were standing in the middle of the living room, silence surrounding them, that she realized how scantily attired she was. Ellen squelched the urge to tighten the sash on her robe. If she did, that might make her seem vulnerable, something she didn't want. What was going on inside her had to remain her secret.

Already this man had the ability to make her think and behave with an abandon she'd never thought possible. While exciting on the one hand, on the other it was downright frightening. She wanted to be in control of her thoughts and actions at all times. Around him, she seemed to lose control of both.

"Did I interrupt anything?" Porter asked, his voice sounding gruff, almost scratchy.

She sensed he was not as nonchalant as she'd first thought. He suddenly seemed as uncomfortable as she felt. But then buying an entire building that cost hundreds of thousands of dollars could have a tendency to complicate most anything.

"Look, if you're here to rehash—"

"I'm not," he interrupted.

She gave him a hard, suspicious look. "Oh."

"Okay, I'll admit that's one of the reasons why I'm here."

She kept quiet, though her mind was clicking, trying to figure out how best to diffuse this lethal situation.

"But not the only one," he hastened to add before she could say anything.

That last statement gave her a start, especially as it was spoken in a low, husky tone. She jerked her eyes up to his, only to wish she hadn't. They were narrowed but filled with an emotion she couldn't identify, or maybe didn't want to.

She steeled herself against the heat that invaded her body. What was there about him that turned her inside out? Whatever it was, it made her want something she'd been content *not* to want, and that was passion.

"Say what you have to say while I'm in the mood to listen," Ellen said at last, tearing her gaze away from his.

When he remained silent, her panic grew, along with the tension. She had to get him out of her house. He seemed different, brooding, serious—a side of him she hadn't seen. He was up to something, only she didn't know what. That unknown frightened her.

"It's not that easy. I'm not the best with words."

"I think you do just fine." Because of that gnawing fear, her words were biting.

His lips quirked at the slam, then sobered, as did his features.

"Why won't you leave me alone?" she blurted out, only to wish she could take the words back. She didn't want to hear his answer. She just wanted him out of her life so she could regain the peace of mind he'd stolen.

He closed the distance between them, though he didn't touch her. Yet she knew he could hear her heart beating in her chest.

"I can't."

"Can't—or won't?" she whispered, licking her lower lip.

She thought she heard a groan escape him, but she couldn't be sure.

"They're one and the same," Porter said.

"I don't understand."

"Yes, you do."

She clamped her lips together. Her worst thoughts

were coming true. They were going to end up arguing again.

"Please, leave me alone," Ellen said, stopping short of begging.

"That's not going to happen, but I can't tell you why."

Ellen shook her head and jutted her chin against the deepening huskiness in his tone. "Why not?"

"I don't have the right words for that, either."

"You're not making sense," she said, growing weary of the conversation. "We're back to where we started—at an impasse."

"No, we're not. Why I'm here makes perfect sense. And even if I can't tell you, I can sure as hell show you."

Ellen's startled eyes bounced back to his face when he reached for her hand and placed it on his crotch. A gasp parted her lips as she felt the hardness even through the fabric of his jeans.

"Damn you," she rasped, fighting off the stinging tears behind her eyelids.

His hand tightened on hers, holding it in place; then, leaning over, he placed his hot mouth against hers. The kiss seemed to dig deep inside and suck every last ounce of resistance out of her.

Ellen sagged against him and clutched at his shirt, reveling in the lashing his tongue was giving hers. Finally he drew back, took a staggering breath and peered down at her with glazed eyes. But he didn't say anything. There wasn't anything to say that hadn't already been said with their lips and tongues.

"You knew this was bound to happen," he whispered at last, taking the liberty of leisurely untying the sash of her robe.

Frozen to the floor at this brazen move, Ellen let her eyes track his as they traveled the length of her body before returning to her breasts where they remained.

"Lovely," he said, circling one with the tip of a callused finger.

To Ellen's dismay, her nipple sprang erect.

He smiled, bent his head and replaced his finger with his tongue. Her neck arched, and her knees would have buckled if he hadn't been holding her up.

"I want you more than I've ever wanted anyone."

"Oh, Porter—"

The unfinished sentence jammed in her throat as he trailed that same finger down her stomach to the crevice at her thighs. When he moved it back and forth there and his finger came back wet, he seemed to lose it.

"To hell with the bedroom," he ground out, shucking out of his clothes.

Ellen's eyes rounded. "Where?"

"Here, on the sofa."

"But...how?" Ellen could barely speak.

"You'll see."

Without further ado, he backed her legs against the sofa. After she was sitting down, he pulled her buttocks to the edge, all the while staring into her eyes.

"Porter, I've never—"

"Shh, trust me. It's okay."

It wasn't that she didn't trust him. At this point in their heated game, trust no longer entered into it. *Sat-*

isfaction was the key issue. Still, she'd never made love like this before, and the idea both frightened and excited her at the same time.

Excitement won.

"Lift your legs," he encouraged.

She did as she was told. Once her legs were positioned on either side of his shoulders, he lifted her buttocks off the sofa and entered her with a strong thrust.

"Ohhh," she cried, digging her fingernails into his forearms, then gave in to the deep, long thrusts. In a matter of seconds she heard his groans as he emptied into her, rocking her with a climax like none she'd ever experienced.

"Ohhh," she cried again, only louder, as the assault on her body continued.

Moments later he slipped out of her, lifted her into his arms and, without asking, made his way down the hall into her bedroom.

Once they were on the bed, he leaned over and kissed her again.

"Porter—"

He placed a finger across her mouth. "Shush, don't say anything. Just enjoy."

Was she ever doing that, especially when his lips attached themselves to a swollen breast. He suckled until she began to squirm, the heat gathering in her and threatening to erupt into another climax.

As if sensing her dilemma, Porter chuckled, then moved to the other breast, where he worked the same magic. Ellen's squirming increased, as did her pleasure.

Porter's eyes glittered as he looked at her before lowering his head to her navel, where he dipped his tongue. Only after his tongue traveled lower and reached the apex of her thighs did she moan out loud.

"Don't hold back," he whispered.

"Oh, please!"

"Please what?"

"Take me!"

Without further hesitation, he rolled onto his back. Before she realized his intentions, he had lifted her and was sliding her down on him. Waves of pleasure washed through her as she felt his burgeoning fullness high inside her.

Flushed and feeling as if she could conquer the world, Ellen grabbed his muscled forearms. Together they moved in concert. It was only when the climax was upon them that she closed her eyes and gave into another sweet/savage attack on her body.

Their cry penetrated the air in unison.

Ellen awakened first.

She didn't have to peer at the space next to her to know that she wasn't alone. She could hear Porter's steady breathing. She hadn't thought she would have a man next to her anytime soon, if ever again.

Yet when it came to Porter, she had known, deep down, that this affair was inevitable. But as the old saying went, no one got past the grim reaper, which in her case didn't mean death, but rather her conscience.

To her way of thinking, making passionate love with someone was supposed to be synonymous with commitment. Heretofore, that had been the case. What had happened to change her mind about such an important moral precept? It wasn't what, but who, she admitted.

Porter Wyman.

He had blindsided her with his lazy gait, his ready smile and his gorgeous body. It had been a fatal attraction from the moment she'd laid eyes on him, though she had refused to face that fact. Now she had to come to terms with that, as he shared both her bed and her body.

"Are you sorry?"

His gruff, sleep-laden voice sent her heart into a nosedive. She turned and faced him. "Are you?"

"I asked first."

"I don't know."

He sighed. "Well, I do. I have no regrets."

"Men never do."

"Hey, don't be that way."

"How do you want me to be?"

"Glad and satisfied."

Ellen had to smile. "I am satisfied. I've never made love that many times in one night."

His eyes darkened. "I don't like to think about you with someone else."

She didn't quite know how to respond to that without knowing where this conversation, this night, would eventually lead.

"Was your ex a good lover?"

"Porter, I—"

"Was he?" Porter pressed, a hint of hot steel in his tone, something she hadn't heard before.

"No." She flushed. "It had to be all his way or not at all."

"Ah, I see." Porter paused and traced her swollen lips with a finger. She trapped it, then licked it with her tongue, drawing a groan from him. "You'd best watch it. I'm already hard again."

She rolled her eyes at which he smiled, but only briefly.

"Were you always satisfied?"

"No," she admitted, her face flaming at his bluntness. "Never, actually."

Porter sucked in his breath. "You're not serious?"

She gave him a troubled look. "I'm serious."

"He must have been an insensitive ass."

"Not at first, or at least I didn't see that side of him. He just didn't know how to—"

"Satisfy you."

"Er…right. Or maybe I never gave him a fair chance. Our first time together was such a disaster that it was never right after that. Eventually he accused me of being frigid."

"Hell, he *is* an ass. You're the hottest, most passionate woman I've ever been with."

"How many other women have you told that to, including your ex?"

"None."

"I don't believe you."

He shrugged, toying with a breast. "It's true. Oh, I won't say that Wanda wasn't good in bed, because she was. But she was the aggressor, wanted it rough and kinky."

"She sounds like a piece of work."

"That's an understatement."

"Then why did you marry her?"

"What can I say? She chased me until she caught me."

"That's too simple an explanation."

"You're right, it is. I thought I loved her. Maybe at one time I really did. But she didn't like being married. Right after the ceremony, that became evident. She wanted to travel and spend money. Did a damn good job of both, too."

"Why did you ever let her get pregnant?"

"Let? Ha! That's a joke. She stopped taking her pills, figured she'd get what she wanted if she had a baby, which was to get me to sell the business and the ranch."

"Apparently her ploy didn't work."

"Nope. I'm generous as they come until I'm pushed into a corner."

"After the baby came, what happened?"

"Just like Meg told you, she didn't like motherhood. I paid her off, and she *took* off."

"Do you think she'll stay gone?"

"She has no choice. But she did call my attorney the other day and ask about Matt."

"That's not a good sign."

"I don't want anything to do with that bitch ever again."

To hear him say that warmed Ellen's heart. "Oh, Porter, what a mess."

He smiled and tweaked a nipple. "My attorney did as he was told and found out what she was up to. Turns out she's remarried and long gone, living in

Canada to be exact. Besides, my custody of Matt is airtight. No one will ever get my son away from me. He comes first.''

At least she'd gleaned one vital tidbit from this coupling. *She* or any other woman would always come second in his life. So what? This night of passion hadn't changed their relationship.

They had gone to bed together and that was all.

''I haven't changed my mind about the building,'' she said without preamble, suddenly not liking herself at all. ''I don't want you to go through with that deal.''

Porter's hand stilled. ''Aw, hell, I don't want to talk about that now.''

''I do.''

''It's too late. The building is mine, lock, stock and barrel.''

Ellen gritted her teeth. ''And was this evening collection time?''

''Dammit, you know better than that.''

''I don't like strings, Porter. Samuel kept me tied, and I hated it.''

''Do you think that's what this was all about, making you beholden because I bought that building?''

''I don't know what to think.''

''Then how 'bout not thinking at all? Please, Ellen, don't ruin what we have.''

''And what is that?''

''Whatever you want it to be.''

''Oh, no, you don't. You're not putting that monkey on my back.''

"Look, we were—are—great in bed. Why can't we just go with the flow and see what happens?"

She moved away from him. "Going with the flow is your way, not mine."

"Then what are you saying?"

"I don't know."

Porter got up and slipped into his jeans. When he was dressed, he strode to the door, then turned. "When you decide, pick up the phone. I'll be around."

Fourteen

Each time the door to the shop opened, Ellen expected to see Porter saunter in. Her expectations were never met. It had been a week since they had made love, and she hadn't seen or heard from him.

Was he punishing her for not making any kind of commitment to him? Or was this his definition of a cooling off period? No, she corrected herself mentally. He'd had the last word, dammit. He'd left the decision to her as to whether she wanted to see him again or not.

Even so, she hadn't thought he would give up so easily. If she'd learned one thing about this man, it was that he was tenacious to a fault.

But maybe he'd decided their relationship was riddled with too many problems and wasn't worth the hassle. After all, he'd been through a horrible experience with one woman. Why should he have anything to do with another one who was lukewarm at best?

Suddenly Ellen's face flamed. Lukewarm, ha! In bed, she'd been anything but that. She had told the truth when she'd admitted to Porter that Samuel had never made love to her with such bold, all-consuming passion.

With Porter, nothing had been held in check. He had given all: his body, his mind, *his soul.* Consequently she'd done the same, never imagining she had that kind of untapped heat inside her.

When he'd backed her against the sofa and taken her there, she'd been transported into sexual heaven; she'd never experienced such a high. Later, when his lips had made their way between her thighs...

Ellen lunged out of the chair behind her desk, her head and stomach reeling. The thought of that moment and the orgasm that had racked her made her ache for more of the same. Now! Then why hadn't she said *yes, yes, yes* when Porter had expressed a desire to be with her again, knowing that she could have had a steady diet of him and his body?

Fear.

She feared losing her identity again. She had been controlled by one man for far too long, and she wasn't ready to entangle herself in another relationship, though Samuel and Porter were nothing alike.

Plus, she hadn't had enough time for herself, to find out who she really was. She'd been what Samuel had wanted and expected her to be, to the extent that she'd lost her own identity.

Now she was beginning to find herself again by enjoying the simple things in life, such as serving someone a cup of coffee and selling a pretty box of stationery. And when the day was over and the shop locked behind her, she could go home and do whatever she felt like doing, without having to please or answer to anyone.

So why was that no longer enough? Porter again. He had bulldozed his way into her life, and when he'd kissed her that first time, she'd been mowed down flat. She hadn't recovered.

Nevertheless, she wasn't ready for another full-blown relationship, having to answer once again to someone else and his needs. If that was selfish, then so be it. She could live with that flaw just fine.

So stop fretting over the fact that you haven't seen Porter, she told herself, getting up and walking into the front, where she paused and looked around. It was early, too early to open, but everything was pristine and ready.

Ellen took a deep breath and filled her lungs with the potent aroma of coffee, which was almost as potent as the smell of Porter in the throes of sex. Feeling as if her face was on fire, she placed her palms on her cheeks. What in the world was happening to her?

She might not want Porter in her life, but she sure as hell wanted him in her bed. While that might not make sense, it was the unvarnished truth.

"Quit behaving like an idiot," she muttered, striding toward a shelf where a grouping of "pretties" wasn't quite right. She eyed them critically for a long moment, then rearranged them.

Just as she finished, the phone rang. It was her sister.

"Morning, Meggy. What's going on?"

"Nothing good, I'm sorry to say."

Ellen's pulse raced. "What's wrong?" She wanted to add *now,* but she refrained, not wanting to appear insensitive.

"I'm looking for a sounding board, someone to bitch to, actually."

"I'm listening."

"It's Ralph. He just called from Wyoming, and we had it out about Kyle."

"Discussing your kid over long distance hardly seems fair," Ellen said, choosing her words carefully.

"You're telling me. I'm thinking seriously of asking the doctor to give Ralph something for his nerves."

"Are you taking your medicine yet?"

"Yes, only now I'm thinking I might start doubling the dose."

"I don't think so."

"Why not? My life's falling apart. And Kyle's mouthing off because he doesn't have a fancy car like his highfalutin running buddies. And money—well, it's in such short supply that I'm nearly nuts jockeying the monthly bills."

"Now, Meg, how many times do I have to tell you that I'll help?"

"No. I'm *not* taking your money."

"Dammit, don't be so hard-headed."

"I could say the same about you."

"This conversation's not about me," Ellen

stressed, then switched the subject before she lost her temper. Hard-headed wasn't the word for Meg. She went beyond that.

"Other than griping, is Kyle behaving?"

"I'm not sure."

"Look, how 'bout I come over?" Ellen asked, thinking the phone was not the right setting for this kind of discussion. "I can leave the shop with—"

"No! Don't do that. I'm okay. In fact, I'd rather be alone."

"Megan, please, don't shut me out."

"I'm not. You know that. It's just that I'm into this pity-party business and rather enjoying it."

Ellen almost laughed. "I can identify with that. I've had a few of them lately myself."

"By the way, what about you and Porter and the building?"

"I haven't decided yet. About the building, that is," Ellen said, ignoring the personal part of the question.

"Talk about hard-headed. If you move out of that location, you need your head examined."

"You've made your point," Ellen said drolly. "Look, I'll talk to you later. Hey, make that pity party brief, okay?"

Ellen heard Meg chuckle before she hung up.

Suddenly problems seemed to be flying at her from every side. She wished there was something she could do for her sister. For starters, she would like to kick Meg's husband and son in the butt. Families meant responsibility, all the more reason for not involving *herself* with another man.

Life was too short.

With that thought up front, Ellen marched to the front door, opened it and greeted her first customer with a false smile.

"Why, good morning, Mrs. Cavanaugh."

"I'm returning what I bought yesterday," she said in her usual nasal and whiny tone.

Figures, you old blue-haired biddy, Ellen thought, even as her smile widened and she said through clenched teeth, "How 'bout a cup of coffee first? On me."

He was a mess.

Porter sighed, got up and, with dragging feet, trudged to the window in his office. Two squirrels were chasing each other through the limbs of a huge oak tree. He watched them for a moment, emptying his mind of everything but them. But that relief was short-lived.

Thoughts of Ellen continued to torment him. He wanted to see her. No, that wasn't a strong enough word. He was desperate to see her, not only to relieve the ongoing hardness in his groin, but to be around her. She had done a number on him.

And he knew why. Underneath that uptight, sometimes icy facade, she was all fire. He'd never felt so good as when he was inside her, thrusting high and deep. Even now, he could hear her moans, her cries as she climaxed, time after time.

To think he could bring her such pleasure made him want her that much more. His fantasy was to make love to her every day for the rest of his life.

Suddenly the area behind his zipper went limp.

Had he fallen in love with her? Oh, Lord, he hoped not, reaching into his pocket and drawing out his handkerchief. Once he'd mopped the sweat off his forehead, Porter felt the sudden tightening in his chest relax somewhat.

If and when he made another commitment, he wanted it to be a lifetime one. He didn't want to go through another Wanda debacle. For nearly two years now he'd held true to his vow not to become involved with another woman, not permanently, that is.

Then along came Ellen Saxton and rang his bell in more ways than one.

"Hey, boss, someone wants to see you."

Porter hadn't even heard George open his door. Jerking around, he scowled at him.

George gave him a startled look. "Man, you look green. Are you sick?"

"What do you want?"

"I told you. There's a lady out front who wants to see you."

Could it be Ellen? Porter's chest tightened again. "Does that lady have a name?"

He shrugged with a grin. "Not that she told me."

"What the hell? Send her on back."

When Megan Drysdale walked into his office, he was stunned, but he didn't let it show.

"I hope you don't mind being interrupted," she said in a hesitant tone.

"No way, not when it's one of my favorite people."

She relaxed visibly. "You're one of the nicest people I know, Porter."

"Maybe that's my problem."

"My sister's a fool."

He laughed. "She wasn't happy about my buying the building, that's for sure."

"I wasn't talking just about the building."

"Oh?"

"Don't 'oh' me. I was referring to something a little more personal. You're a damn good catch."

Her bluntness brought on a hearty chuckle. "Well, actually, I think you're right, but we'll let that be our secret. For now, anyway."

They both laughed, which he noticed lessened the strained look on her face. Something was wrong. Thank goodness it apparently had nothing to do with Ellen, which had been his first thought.

"Have a seat and tell me what's on your mind."

"What are you doing here?"

It was closing time, and she had been about to turn the key in the lock when she'd looked up and saw Porter standing there, grinning as if nothing had happened between them. Her blood pressure shot up, as did her temper. Would she ever understand what made this man tick? Probably not, since she wasn't going to try.

Now, as she confronted him, his grin tempered into a smile. "Two reasons why I'm here," he said, stepping inside.

Ellen leaned against the counter. He followed, stopping a hairsbreadth from her. In fact, his breathing fanned her face, making her knees tremble slightly. "I'm listening."

"Number one, your sister came to see me today, and I hired her to work for me."

Ellen straightened. "You didn't!"

"Sure did. And number two, I *had* to see you."

Ellen's mind scrambled to take in his sultry spoken words. "Why...I mean...?"

His hot, seeking mouth gave her the answer. When the burning kiss finally ended and she regained her ability to catch her breath, she stared up at him. "You don't exactly play fair, do you?"

He angled his head and smiled. "Nope. But then, I never said I did."

Porter leaned over and ran his tongue over her mouth, retracing where his lips had been. "Every time I get near you, I get hard."

"Please." She went weak all over.

"Please what?" he whispered. "Please rip your clothes off and take you on the spot?"

"Is that what you want?"

He covered a breast. "More than you'll ever know."

"What's stopping you?" she asked in a breathless voice.

The phone rang.

An expletive spewed from his lips. "That damn thing's stopping me, but only if you answer it."

She was tempted not to, but since the mood was broken, she scooted out of his arms, dashed to the buffet and picked up the receiver.

"Oh, God, Ellen, Kyle's been arrested!" Meg cried in her ear.

Fifteen

"**W**hat if he doesn't get him out?" Meg sniffled into the tissue in her hand. But when she looked back up at Ellen, her eyes were brimming with tears.

Ellen was sitting next to her sister on the sofa thirty minutes after Meg's hysterical call. She and Porter had jumped into his truck and driven straight to the Drysdales'. Once inside, Porter had taken charge in his calm and reassuring manner.

"Shh, hush that up, you hear?" he'd told Meg. "Everything's going to be all right."

"It'll never be all right again," Meg had wailed. "When Ralph finds out about this, he'll go bonkers."

Porter had one of Meg's hands in his. Ellen had the other. They squeezed at the same time. It was Porter, however, who continued to console her.

"Don't worry about Ralph right now. Just try to get hold of yourself and tell us what happened."

"I'm not sure. Before I called Ellen, I got a call from the police saying Kyle had been arrested along with several other boys. They had all been drinking."

"Oh no," Ellen murmured, squeezing Meg's hand harder. She hated this latest development but wasn't surprised. Kyle was rebellious at the best of times, partly because Meg was too easy on him and partly because Ralph was never home to do what fathers were supposed to do.

The main problem was finances, or the lack thereof. And Meg was too proud to accept help. But now that she was going to work for Porter part-time, maybe she could at least buy Kyle a decent car. However, it seemed that lacking a "cool" vehicle was the least of her nephew's problems. Getting arrested certainly took precedence over that.

"Juvenile detention said they would release him to a parent," Meg was saying.

"But you hate to go alone, right?" Ellen asked.

"I think it'd be better if I went," Porter said. "You call and leave permission for me to pick Kyle up."

"Oh, would you?" Meg asked in a broken tone.

Ellen's heart went out to her, but she was powerless to do anything, which increased her frustration. Damn that kid.

"You bet. I'll do whatever it takes."

Porter stood. Ellen felt his eyes on her. She looked up. Their gazes locked for a moment; then Porter nodded, tipped his hat and walked out.

Every time he looked at her that way, as if he could

eat her with a spoon, it left her feeling weak and confused. She wanted this man, yet she didn't want to want him, which made no sense at all.

What a quandary, made even more so by his involvement with her family. He seemed to be trying to ingratiate himself in their lives so that none of them would be able to do without him. Was that a ploy directed at her, to convince her that *she* couldn't do without him, that she *needed* him in her life?

No. After all, he hadn't made any commitment to her. They had made love, but that hadn't come with strings attached.

"Ellen, how did I fail so badly as a mother?"

Ellen shook herself out of her reverie. "Baloney. You haven't failed. It's the times. Kids are living in the fast lane. Some can handle it. Others can't."

"Kyle wants all the high-priced things his friends have, and we simply can't afford them. Half the time Ralph's on the road or holed up somewhere 'cause his rig's in a repair shop."

"And when he's not moving, he's not making money?"

"Exactly."

"What do you think triggered Kyle's latest escapade?"

"Janis broke up with him."

"Uh-oh."

Meg blew her nose, then tossed the tissue into the wastebasket. "I'm sure it's because his old car broke down and he couldn't take her out any longer. But I'm not sorry about that. After what happened in your shop, I've been afraid. Janis is much too sophisticated for him.''

"You're right. He needs to be dating someone more his own age.''

"So do you think they'll let Porter bring him home?''

"If it can be done, he'll do it. So stop worrying until you know what you have to worry about. I'm sure they'll be walking in that door soon.''

And they were. During her and Meg's second round of coffee, Porter, followed by a hangdog Kyle, strode into the house.

"Have you had anything to eat?'' Meg asked first off.

"Yes, ma'am.''

"Then go to your room.'' Meg's voice was quiet but firm. "We'll talk later.''

Once Kyle was gone, Meg gave Porter her full attention. "Is he—''

"Going to jail?'' Porter sort of smiled. "No. Since he's a minor, the situation's different. The probation officer wants him on informal probation.''

"Oh, Porter, thank you, thank you. I don't know what I'd...we'd do without you.''

"I hope you don't ever have to.'' Porter cut his eyes to Ellen, and to her dismay, she felt her cheeks burn. "And you're more than welcome.''

"How 'bout some coffee?''

"Not for me, thanks,'' Porter said, once again focusing his eyes on Ellen.

She stood and leaning over, kissed Meg on top of

the head. "If you're okay, we'll be going. You need to spend time with your son."

Meg rose also. "That's an understatement. Thanks again, Porter, for everything. And you, too, sis."

"Don't thank me. I didn't do anything."

"And you needn't thank me, either," Porter added. "Just show up at the store when you can and help us out."

"You know I'll do that."

"By the way, how do you feel about Kyle going to work after school? I could help out there."

Meg didn't hesitate. "That would be nice. I've never encouraged him to get a job." Meg paused, tearing up again. "I wanted him to enjoy his school days, thinking he'd have the rest of his life to work. But it apparently wasn't the right call."

Porter reached out and patted her on the shoulder. "Keep your chin up, you hear?"

"I'll try."

Ellen kissed her again. "I'll be in touch. Call if you need me."

Porter whipped the truck into Ellen's driveway and killed the engine. Her car was still at the shop, and she didn't care. She would make arrangements for Janis to pick her up in the morning.

The two of them remained silent, as they'd been from the time they had left her sister's. Surprisingly the lack of conversation hadn't been awkward.

Ellen guessed she'd been too self-focused, her mind jumping all over the map. She was incredibly weary, yet restless at the same time.

Perhaps it was that restlessness that prompted her to ask, "Would you like to come in?"

"Sure, but aren't you too tired?"

"Yes and no."

Porter grinned and shook his head. "Makes perfect sense to me. Let's go."

Moments later, they were inside the house. Porter removed his Stetson and tossed it on a chair, then sat on the sofa. Ellen looked on, thinking his fit body seemed to take up all the space. More than that, he seemed to belong there. A warning bell clanged inside her head.

What was he thinking? That maybe she'd invited him in for the night? And had she? Was that what this was all about? No. She wanted to find out about Kyle and to thank him for helping. That was her reason and nothing else. To make love with him again would not be smart. Nothing had changed to make her think they had a future together.

"Want some more coffee?" she asked, suddenly unsure of herself, an emotion she'd sworn she would never feel after ditching Samuel.

"Thanks, I'll pass. As it is, my insides are doing handsprings from so much caffeine."

"Mine, too."

"So sit down. I'm not going to pounce on you."

Ellen blushed. "Dammit, why is it you can read my mind?"

"I'd have to be dumber than a box of rocks not to see how skittish you are."

"You haven't lost your way with words."

He gave her a lopsided smile. "Don't aim to."

"So where do we go from here?" she asked into the taut silence.

If possible, his eyes turned darker. "That's up to you."

"I don't want to make that call."

"Then I will. I want you. But then, you know that."

"Porter—"

"Save it," he said on a sigh. "I'm aware that you're not into having an affair."

Ellen shifted her gaze. "Right."

"Then we're back to square one. We want each other with no strings or commitments. But since you don't want an affair, how do we pull that off?"

"I don't—"

The obtrusive sound of the phone stopped her words.

Porter turned and glared at the persistent instrument. "That sonofabitch ought to be jerked out of the wall."

While Porter was furious at the untimely interruption, she was relieved. Panic was playing havoc with her insides. She crossed the room and picked up the receiver, only to catch her breath and hold her silence.

"Ellen, you still there?"

"Yes."

Porter jumped up and mouthed, "Is it Meg?"

Ellen shook her head. Although he didn't say anything else, that dark look remained intact as she felt his eyes bore into her.

"What do you want, Samuel?" she demanded, her gaze on Porter.

He seemed to freeze; then his eyes narrowed, as did his mouth.

"You don't sound glad to hear from me," her ex said in a petulant tone.

"I'm not."

"Okay, Ellen, you've had your fun."

"Trust me, talking to you is not fun."

"Hey, I thought we parted friends."

She ignored that and asked, "Why did you call?"

"To ask when you're coming back to Tyler."

"I don't know."

"I was hoping to see you."

"That's not a good idea. What could we possibly have to say to each other?"

"You might not have anything to say to me, but I have something to say to you."

"Then say it now, over the phone."

"No can do."

For a long moment Ellen held her silence. The last thing she'd expected or wanted was a call from her ex, especially with Porter standing there glaring at her, a fighting expression on his face. Porter aside, she didn't want to see or talk to Samuel herself. Those days were over.

"When *are* you coming to Tyler?"

"Not anytime soon."

"When you do, will you call me?"

"Samuel, I don't—"

"Please."

"I'll think about it. That's the best I can do."

Samuel hung up, and she kept her eyes on Porter. If anything, his features were grimmer than ever.

"What did that bastard want?" he asked.

"He wouldn't say."

"Well, he sure as hell said something."

"He wants to talk to me."

"I bet he does."

"Hey, why are you getting so uptight? He's my problem, not yours. If I see him, it's because I don't trust him. He could be up to something."

"Don't do it."

"See him, you mean?"

"Damn straight. I don't want you going back to Tyler."

Ellen stared at him, wide-eyed, while her heart upped its beat. "That's not your call."

Suddenly and without warning, Porter reached out and pulled her against the length of him. That action left no doubt as to the state he was in. The hardness below his belt dug into her stomach as he latched onto the cheeks of her buttocks and ground her against him.

The breath swished out of her at the same time that his lips found hers, giving her a hard, wet kiss.

"What…what was that all about?" she whispered inanely, then backed up, out of harm's reach.

Porter's eyes narrowed, then glittered into hers. "You figure it out. But just in case you don't, you're *mine* now. You tell the bastard that—or I will."

With that, he walked out and slammed the door.

For the longest time, Ellen remained in place, her mouth quivering and her mind reeling.

Sixteen

Porter had mentally knocked himself around more times than he cared to count. He couldn't believe he'd actually gone that far out on the proverbial limb and declared that Ellen was his.

You're mine! You're mine! You're mine!

Those words rattled around in his mind like loose marbles until his head pounded. Now that he thought about that moment again, he was sure he'd sounded like some modern day Tarzan.

What a jerk.

Ellen had probably wanted to throw up. Maybe she had, after he'd walked out of her house. Suddenly his own stomach felt queasy, something that rarely ever happened to him. What had driven him to make that bold statement?

Lust, not love, remained the culprit. He'd been

thinking with his lower anatomy instead of his upper, which would get a man in trouble every time.

Even though he'd opened his mouth and inserted his big boot, Porter realized he couldn't stay away from her indefinitely. It had been three days since that mess with her sister's kid. To him, it seemed like three months.

Thank goodness he'd been able to pull enough strings to get Kyle out of immediate trouble, although the kid would have to do a lot of hours of community service to make up for getting caught in the car with a can of beer in his hand.

Meg and Ralph, who was finally home, had called and thanked him profusely for his intervention. Hopefully things would improve around the Drysdale household.

Ellen and her thoughts were all that concerned him. That was why he was headed to the coffee shop. He'd stayed away from her for as long as he could. Even if he didn't do anything but look at her, he would be okay. He was hungry for the sight of her.

"You're sick, Wyman," he murmured, wheeling the truck into the only empty space in front of Coffee, Anyone? The air was thick and inviting with the aroma of freshly brewed coffee. He took a deep breath, then let it out.

When he did, the animal in the seat beside him woke up.

"Hey, fellow." He reached over and rubbed the dog behind the ears. "Want to go inside with me?"

The dog, who was just a dog and nothing more,

wagged both his tongue and his tail. "Let's you and me be about our business, then."

Porter strode inside a shop that was indeed buzzing, not only with satisfied coffee drinkers but shoppers, as well. A part of him was glad about the success of Ellen's endeavor, while another part wasn't. Hell, he wasn't ever going to try to figure out what that asinine thought was all about, much less where it would lead.

Shaking his head, he moved on.

"She's in the courtyard, Mr. Wyman," a young woman behind the counter said, her eyes focused on the panting dog in his arms.

Porter could read her thoughts as if she'd spoken them; they said: no dogs allowed. He agreed, but he wasn't planning to stay long, and he couldn't leave the newest addition to his family outside in a hot vehicle.

"Thanks," he said, nodding at several women who had traded at his store.

He stepped out into the courtyard just as Ellen headed back inside. She stopped beside the active fountain and stared open-mouthed. He didn't know which shocked her more—seeing him, or seeing the dog in his arms. Probably a bit of both, he told himself, feeling a smile spread across his face.

Damn, but she was pretty, dressed in a pair of slacks and a fancy T-shirt that called attention to her rounded breasts, breasts that he'd suckled and...

Cursing silently, he lopped off that thought just as she finally moved and walked up to him.

"Hi," he said, giving her what he hoped was his most disarming grin.

"I can't believe this is for real."

Although he suspected her lips wanted to break into an answering smile, they didn't.

"Me, or the dog?" he quipped, feeling the patrons drinking coffee at the tables focus on them.

"Well, since you put it that way, both."

"I'm here to invite you to a birthday party." Porter decided to act as if nothing out of the ordinary had happened between them, that he hadn't behaved like a jealous lover in heat.

"Whose?"

"Matt's."

Her eyes brightened. "Oh."

"Is that all you have to say?"

"When is it?"

"Tomorrow."

Ellen bit down on her lower lip, something he wished she wouldn't do. God, everything this woman did turned him on.

"All right," she said hesitantly, her gaze concentrated on the dog in his arms. "Animals aren't allowed in the shop, you know."

"I figured as much."

This time her lips did break into a smile. "Is she for Matt?"

"He's for Matt."

"What's his name?"

"For the moment, it's Dog."

She laughed outright, which made him want to kiss her mocha-colored lips all the more. Ellen seemed to sense his thoughts; her breath caught, and their eyes met.

That was when it happened, suddenly and without warning. A squirrel in the oak tree close to the fountain chose that moment to jump from one limb to another.

Dog bounded out of his arms and straight into the fountain. Water splashed everywhere.

"Oh no!" Ellen yelped, jumping back.

"Damn you, Dog, get back here!" Porter reached for the animal, but his efforts were too little, too late. Dog was determined, fountain or no fountain, to get that squirrel.

Dog ran through the water, dousing everyone around him. Customers bounded to their feet, but not before getting drenched.

"Porter!" Ellen cried. "If you don't catch that…that thing, you're going to die a slow, painful death!"

"Come here, you mutt," Porter called, trying to catch the crazed dog as it continued to wreak havoc in its desperation to reach the squirrel.

Porter's efforts were for naught.

"Porter!" Ellen cried again. "Do something!"

"Dammit, I'm trying."

The second those words left his mouth, Dog gave up the chase and jumped on the wide ledge of the fountain.

"Oh, my heavens!"

Porter swung around and watched in horror as Dog proceeded to shake himself, shooting water from his coat all over a woman who seemed to have appeared out of nowhere.

"Oh, Mrs. Cavanaugh, I'm so sorry," Ellen cried,

dashing up to her. After glaring at Porter, she grabbed a napkin and began rubbing one of the dark stains on the older woman's blouse.

"I should think so!" Ruth Cavanaugh exclaimed in a most self-righteous tone, snatching the cloth out of Ellen's hand. "Let me be."

Looking on, Porter watched the old bat's sagging chin quiver and her breasts heave. What he really wanted was to do some *snatching* himself, and that was to remove what little hair she had left in her head.

Instead, he curbed his temper, held on to the wet animal and stepped into the conversation with a smile. "I'm sorry, ma'am, it's all my fault. I'll take full responsibility for any damage."

Porter sensed that Mrs. Cavanaugh was clearly flattered by his apology and attention, but furious with Ellen.

"Well, sir, I don't hold you responsible."

"You should, ma'am, 'cause this mutt's mine. I'm the one who let him get out of control." He upped his smile a degree.

Mrs. Cavanaugh's face bloomed with color. "Well, if you say so."

"I do. You just let me know how much your cleaning costs." He turned and smiled at the others who were watching him. "The same goes for all of you."

With that, Porter grabbed Ellen by the arm and propelled her toward the shop, but not before turning and noticing that everything and everyone had settled down.

"You're something else," Ellen spat, once they were in her office.

"Look, I'm sorry, okay. I screwed up."

"That's one way of putting it." Her tone dripped with sarcasm.

He grinned. "Okay, do I cut my throat now or later?"

She didn't return his grin. "I'd prefer now."

"Got a knife?"

Ellen gritted her teeth. "Take that dog and get out of here. Now."

"Only if you'll come to the party."

"I'll come, I'll come. I'll agree to anything just to get rid of you and your furry friend."

"Good." He leaned over and kissed her parted lips. "See ya."

"It seems my son's taken quite a liking to you."

Ellen smiled up at Porter from her position on the sofa, where she was bouncing a laughing Matt on one knee.

"Ah, it's nice to see you smile again and to know I'm out of the doghouse." Porter paused and grinned. "No pun intended, of course."

"Of course," Ellen responded in her driest tone.

The party had already been in high gear when she had arrived an hour ago. Common sense had told her that she was crazy for coming, but since she had, she intended to enjoy herself.

Porter had met her at the door with Matt in his arms. He'd introduced her to a few neighbors and friends, some of whom had patronized her shop.

Then, once they were alone, she'd given Matt his present, a stuffed animal. Afterward, to her surprise, the baby had reached out his arms to her. With her heart pounding and her eyes on Porter, she'd taken him. He'd been with her ever since. However, she was smart enough to figure out that it was the toy rather than she herself that had Matt entranced.

From time to time she had seen Bonnie's eyes shoot daggers her way, but so far, the housekeeper had kept her distance.

"Speaking of dogs, where is that…that mutt?" Ellen asked, reeling her thoughts back in.

"Outdoors."

"Does Matt like his new pet?"

"Are you kidding? It was love on second sight."

"Second sight?"

He tweaked his son's ear. "Yeah, on first sight, Matt grabbed Dog's tail and yanked."

"Uh-oh."

"So he and I had a counseling session on how we handle our pets."

"Ah, I see."

"They've been best buddies ever since."

"That makes my day."

Porter's lips twitched. "I'm sure it does."

For a moment their gazes locked, and Ellen held her breath as she saw the unsuppressed fire leap into his. He was remembering the time they'd made love, she knew. He wanted her again; she knew that, too. Suddenly a warmth pooled between her legs, the words *you're mine* bouncing around in her head.

She didn't know what he'd meant when he said that, nor did she know now. She suspected those words had been loosely spoken, so she'd tried her best not to dwell on them, for more reasons than one.

"So you ready for some cake and ice cream?" Porter asked after clearing his throat as though it was sore.

"No, but you go ahead."

"I can't believe my son's already two years old."

"He's entering the 'terrible twos.'"

"And I'm looking forward to every minute of it, though he'll probably get his rear paddled more times than one."

"You're a good dad."

Porter's eyes smoldered. "You'd make an even better mom."

Ellen sucked in her breath as the air seemed to fill with a new kind of tension. Somehow she had to diffuse both it and his words.

Porter cursed. "That's not going to happen."

"I—"

The cell phone in her purse chose that instant to ring.

Porter cursed again. "What's the deal with the phone? It seems to haunt us."

Ellen agreed, but she still grabbed it and said hello. She listened for a moment before saying, "You can't. I won't let you. Look, I can't talk now. I'll call you back later, okay?"

She punched the Off button with shaking fingers.

"Was that Samuel bothering you again?"

"No."

"Then who was it? You're as white as a sheet."

Her knee-jerk reaction was to say it was none of

his business, but she didn't. She curbed her tongue and said instead, "It was Liz Sample, the woman who manages my shop in Tyler."

"And?"

"She's quitting."

"Which means what?"

Her impatience showed. "That should be obvious. I have to go to Tyler and find a replacement."

"I suppose you'll see Samuel while you're there?"

"Where's this leading?"

"I wish you wouldn't."

Enough was enough. "Just what *would* you suggest I do?"

There was a moment of profound silence.

"Stay here and marry me."

Seventeen

What time was it?

Ellen stared at the clock on the wall in the living room for the umpteenth time. Twelve o'clock. Still, she wasn't tired enough to sleep. In fact, she hadn't even gone to bed. Since she'd walked in the door from the birthday party, she'd been cleaning house.

Unfortunately there was nothing left to clean. Everything in the entire house sparkled. Maybe she should use the remainder of her nervous energy cleaning the shop.

What she *should* do was face her problems instead of escaping them by running her body into the ground. Besides, it wasn't her body that was her trouble but rather her mind.

Had Porter really asked her to marry him?

Weak, Ellen sank onto the sofa and leaned her head

back. Though she still couldn't believe it, she had indeed heard the proposal, and she was as dumbstruck now as she'd been then.

To make matters worse, she hadn't had a chance to respond, because they had been interrupted. Later, when they could have talked, she'd been too chicken and had avoided him until she could leave without attracting attention to herself.

What to do? What did she *want* to do? That was the real question. Not only did she have to make a decision about his proposal, but she had to find a replacement for Liz at the shop in Tyler. Both were important and weighed heavy on her heart, the proposal topping the list.

Had lust prompted the offer? Or had he really been serious? If it had been the latter, wouldn't he have trapped her and made her give him an answer? He was as obsessive about getting what he wanted as she was, though they went about it in different ways.

She moved like a Texas tornado. He moved like a gentle summer breeze.

But personalities and obsessions aside, there was one tiny factor that hadn't been addressed: Matthew. Ellen's heart jolted at the thought of taking on the responsibility of rearing another woman's child.

She grabbed her stomach. It was while she was bent over that she heard the noise. She jerked her head up and listened. Someone was outside her door. Panic increased the pangs in her belly.

Slowly she got up and went to the door, where she stopped and listened, her heart in her throat.

* * *

Perspiration oozed from his every pore. Porter had reached Ellen's front porch, but he hadn't rung the doorbell yet.

His smile lacked humor. When he did ring and she answered, she would probably slam the door in his face. If only they hadn't been interrupted the second after he'd blurted out his proposal of marriage.

Of all people to intrude, it had to be Bonnie. She'd touched him on the shoulder, telling him that Matt had started ripping into his presents.

He and Ellen had had no choice but to join the fun. Then, the next thing he knew, Ellen was saying good-bye in front of everyone. He'd been tempted to follow her out the door, only to think better of it.

Anyway, it had been obvious that she wanted to avoid both him and the subject of marriage. That was the reason he was standing on her porch at this ungodly hour of the night. No way could he sleep until the matter was settled. What he had to say couldn't wait.

"So push the damn bell and get it over with," he told himself aloud.

He did, which meant it was too late to turn back now.

The lights were on which meant she wasn't asleep. Even so, he figured she wouldn't be happy to see him. Yet he wasn't budging; he wanted an answer, and he wanted it now.

While he was preparing his speech, he heard her ask in an unsteady voice, "Who's there?"

"Porter."

"Do you know what time it is?" she snapped.

"Sure do," he drawled.

"What do you want?"

"Let me in and I'll tell you."

She jerked the door open, and for a moment silence reigned, giving the crickets a free stage to hold their concert. Somehow the sound was comforting, overshadowing the strain that stretched between them.

"I had to see you," Porter said lamely, "to finish what we started."

"Which is?" she asked, holding on to the doorknob.

His eyes darkened. "Don't play coy with me."

"Why not?"

Her teasing tone had mellowed into a husky murmur, which made him hotter than ever. But he saw that as a good sign. At least she hadn't told him to go to hell.

But she hadn't let him in, either. Nevertheless, he felt that she cared about him, maybe even loved him. Miracles did happen.

If not, he didn't know what he would do.

"Teasing me at this point will get you into trouble." His eyes probed hers.

Ellen's tongue traced her bottom lip, leaving a bit of moisture on it. He couldn't let it stay there. Leaning over, he licked it off with his own tongue.

Wordlessly she swayed into him. That was all he needed. "To hell with talking," he said. "We have more pressing business to take care of."

"I agree," she whispered in a wobbly tone.

Attaching his lips to hers once again, Porter backed

her into the house, kicking the door shut behind him with a booted foot.

Moments later, clothes were piled in a heap in the middle of the bedroom floor as they dove for the bed, not even bothering to toss back the spread.

Porter didn't—*couldn't*—wait. He was so hard he feared he might explode. He wanted to be inside her at all costs.

Proposing marriage a second time, something he had sworn would never happen, not only made him nervous, but hotter than hell to boot.

His mouth meshed with hers, and their tongues got reacquainted, while his hands did the same thing, finding the secret places on her body.

When they were both panting hard and their kisses had become frantic, he pushed her legs apart and was about to enter her, only she shook her head.

He stopped, feeling as if she'd slugged him.

"Not to worry," she said in a heated murmur. "It's your turn."

"I don't understand."

"You will."

She forced him on his back and leaned over him. Her tongue was hot and moist and seemed to know exactly where to strike, and strike it did. It laved each nipple until it was hard before dipping into his navel and swirling.

Porter bucked and spoke incoherently. That didn't stop her. The assault continued until she surrounded him with her mouth.

"*Ohhh,*" he moaned, grabbing her hair and lifting her head.

Ellen's eyes, when they met his, were wide and confused. "Am I doing something wrong?"

"Heavens, no," he rasped. "You're doing everything right. It's just that I can't hold back any longer."

Her features cleared as she whispered, "Then I guess we'd best take care of that."

Before he had the chance to make another move, she swung one leg over his lower body. He moaned again as her rich, tight moistness enveloped him, and she began to move. "Oh, yes, yes," he said in a voice he barely recognized as his own.

His hands shot up to her full, damp breasts, which still bore the moistness from his mouth. He increased the tempo, his thrust becoming longer and harder.

Seconds later they both moaned, as one climax followed another. When they were spent, he rolled her over onto her side.

"That was so good," she whispered.

"The best." He pushed the damp hair off her forehead so he could get a better look at her glazed eyes.

"What's wrong?" she asked. "You seem—" she broke off, then went on "—odd. That's the word that comes to mind."

"I'm just wondering where you learned to use your mouth like that."

Her face turned beet red, but her eyes never wavered. "I...don't know. With you, I seem to lose all my inhibitions."

"You never did to Samuel what you did to me?"

Horror now colored her eyes. "Never!"

"Thank God. The thought of that makes me want to kill."

"Even if I'd wanted to, Sam wouldn't have had any part of it. He didn't believe in foreplay or experimentation."

"Straight and narrow to the bitter end."

"And cold."

"I'd say he was an idiot to let the best thing that ever happened to him get away."

"That's a nice thing to say," she said in a husky voice.

"I wasn't being nice. I was being truthful."

She leaned into him and pressed her lips against his. Feeling his head spin from the sheer sweetness of her, he parted her legs and eased two fingers inside her.

"Mmm," she moaned against his lips.

"You're still wet."

He felt her hands encircle him again, and he melted inside.

"And you're still hard."

"So what are we waiting for?" he whispered, turning her onto her back.

She smiled up at him as he replaced his fingers with his hardness, then began a slow rocking of their bodies.

"I'll never get enough of this."

"Me, either."

Their climaxes when they came were quick and hard, their cries simultaneously filling the air.

Porter rubbed his stomach and stared at her through lazy eyes. "Damn but you're a good cook."

Ellen smiled and quirked a delicately arched eyebrow. "You sound surprised."

"Frankly I am."

"Why?"

Porter shrugged. "Standing in front of a stove just doesn't seem to be your thing."

They had finally gone to sleep, and after awakening had taken a shower together, each washing the other, another erotic experience that she wouldn't have missed for anything.

Afterward, both admitting they were ravenous, Ellen had made her way into the kitchen to make breakfast. They had consumed a fair amount of eggs, bacon and biscuits.

"Well, I have to admit, I don't make a habit of it."

"In other words, I was right. It's not your favorite thing."

"Not even close."

He laughed. "Well, when we're married, you will cook some, won't you?"

Married!

That word again. Goose bumps danced across her skin, and her mouth went dry.

"I love you, Ellen. You must know that."

She swallowed hard. "No, no, I don't."

He shoved his chair back, got up and walked to where she stood in front of the sink, her arms crossed over her chest. He peered deep into her eyes, holding her captive.

"Do you love me?"

Did she? The answer came suddenly and with a clarity that almost buckled her knees. "Yes."

"Simple but direct." He kissed her hard. Then, raising his head, he added, "I like that."

"You'd like anything about now."

He smiled as he traced a finger down one side of her cheek. "You're right. But it seems that I stay hard when I'm around you."

"You're incorrigible," she whispered, suddenly moving out of his reach. She couldn't discuss something as important as love and marriage with him so close. His big, warm body robbed her of all perspective and sound judgment.

As if he could read her mind, Porter sighed, then said, "Smart move. We should forget the hanky-panky for a while." He paused. "So, are you willing to take me and my kid on for life?"

She chewed on her lip. "You have to know that motherhood and aprons have never been my thing, either."

"Did I ever say I wanted a woman who wore an apron?"

"You came damn close to that when you asked me if I was willing to cook," she shot back.

"Ah, that was a joke."

"You say that now."

"You calling me a liar?"

"Okay, don't get in a huff."

"Who's in a huff?"

Silence fell over the room for a moment.

"Look, Ellen, I love you and want to marry you. And I'll do everything in my power to make you happy."

"I know."

"I don't even expect you to take care of Matt. Hell, Bonnie can stay on."

"I don't think that would work."

"Why not?"

"I've tried to tell you, and you won't listen. She's in love with you."

"That's not true."

"Yes, it is."

"Then we'll hire someone else."

"None of this is that simple, Porter."

"Why the hell isn't it?"

Ellen didn't hesitate. "I'm afraid."

"Of what?"

"Of making another commitment, and you should be, too."

"I've dumped the past. I'm ready to move on with you, *only you*. That's how simple it is for me, but then, I'm not a complicated man. Never have been, never will be."

"Maybe I am." In spite of her efforts to hold it steady, Ellen felt her mouth tremble.

"So where does that leave us?"

"I need time to get my affairs in order."

"Meaning?"

"Meaning I have to get things squared away in Tyler, find someone to manage the shop." She paused and took a deep breath. "Then maybe I can think about marriage."

His face turned white, and his lips stretched into a thin line. "Your order of priorities stink."

"Excuse me?"

"You heard me, dammit. If you loved me the way

I love you, you sure as hell wouldn't leave. And you wouldn't be worrying about business right now, either.''

Ellen held her temper in check by almost biting her tongue in two. "You're being unreasonable. You of all people should understand the importance of making a living.''

That last statement seemed to set him off. His face turned even whiter, and his words were harsh and cutting. "Know what I think?''

Ellen kept silent.

"I think you want to see your ex.''

Flabbergasted and angry, Ellen lashed back, "That's the most ridiculous thing I've ever heard. And you know better.''

"Do I?''

"Well, if you don't, then our relationship's dead in the water. Because if there's no trust, then there's nothing.''

"Trust has to be earned.''

That tore it. "Okay, so maybe I don't like being pushed into a corner. And maybe I need some breathing room. Or maybe I can't face the idea of marrying again right now. Maybe not ever.''

"If you leave, you won't come back.''

"Are you saying I have to choose between you and my work?''

Porter was quiet for a long moment, though he never flinched or removed his deep-seated gaze. "Yeah, I guess that's what I'm saying.''

"Then you'd better forget about me. No man— including you— is ever going to run roughshod over me again.''

Eighteen

***

"**Y**ou're getting married?"

Samuel peered at her with a smug expression on his face. "No, I *am* married."

By sheer force of will, Ellen remained seated in her chair in the restaurant, though what she wanted was to jump up and sing the hallelujah chorus. Instead she gave her ex-husband a smile, then said, "Congratulations. I hope she'll make you a happy man for the rest of your life."

Samuel's perfect, too perfect, features broke into a brief smile, which was something rare for him. Ellen always thought that if he laughed out loud his perfect face would crack.

God, she pitied the poor woman who had gotten stuck with him, but maybe she was as anal as he was. If so, they had truly found their heaven on earth.

"So what about you?" Samuel asked, breaking into her reverie. "I presume you didn't come back to Tyler just to see me."

"You presumed right," Ellen said with brutal candor. In the past, she'd felt compelled to weigh her responses for fear of setting him off on a tirade. Thank God those days were long gone; she was a liberated woman, and it felt good.

"Are you happy?"

"Do you really care, Sam?"

He shrugged.

She smirked. "So your big news was to tell me you were married. You could've done that over the phone."

"Probably, but for some reason I thought we should see each other one more time."

Ellen smiled with no warmth, then stood. "Well, you thought wrong. Goodbye, Sam."

Before he could make a comeback, she turned and walked out.

That conversation had taken place yesterday at noon, which was one more thing she could cross off her list since returning to the place she considered home.

Now, as she walked around her coffee shop, she experienced an unexpected and unwanted pang of homesickness for Nacogdoches. Or was that pang linked to Porter?

Porter.

Just thinking about him turned her legs to water and sent her heart nosediving. Sinking into the nearest chair, she stared outside. Immediately after Porter had walked out, she had cried until she couldn't cry anymore. Shortly after she'd gotten control of her splattered emotions, Meg had called.

Ellen had given her a blow-by-blow account of what had happened, and Meg had been concerned. When she'd told her sister she was going to Tyler for a while, Meg had encouraged her to do so.

Ellen sensed, however, that Meg didn't approve of the way she'd handled her affairs, having become a true champion of Porter. But Meg's devotion was understandable. After all, Porter had gotten Kyle out of trouble and given Meg a much-needed job. Hence, life at the Drysdale house had greatly improved. Kyle had straightened out, and Ralph was off the road to stay.

Too bad her own fairy tale hadn't had the same wonderful ending. But Porter had wanted more from her than she was prepared to give.

Still, Ellen hadn't wallowed in self-pity to the extent that she hadn't gotten anything done. Since arriving in Tyler, she'd accomplished her goals. She'd met with Sam, and she'd hired a new manager for the shop.

Liz had introduced her to a wonderful older lady who had retail experience galore and knew how to cook the most delicious low-fat meals. After visiting with her for several hours, Ellen hired Nancy Maze on the spot and knew she had a winner.

Although she hadn't changed her mind, Ellen wondered what she was going to do. She hated to admit it, but she'd never been more miserable in her life.

"Hey you, what's up?"

Ellen swung around and stared at her friend Liz Sample, who had let herself in the back office door. It was Sunday, and the shop was closed.

"What makes you think anything's up?"

"Because you look like someone just died."

Ellen made a face at her long-time friend. "You have such a way with words." Like someone else I know, she was tempted to add, but didn't. Dredging up thoughts of Porter only depressed her more.

Liz laughed. "I know."

"Get some coffee and sit down."

Once Liz had done just that, she asked, "Want to talk?"

"There's nothing to talk about," Ellen hedged.

"I'm not buying that."

"Okay, so there's lots to talk about."

Liz propped her hands under her chin and stared at Ellen. "Shoot. I've got all afternoon."

He had behaved like an ass.

That thought and others, equally as colorful, darted through Porter's mind as he headed his horse in the direction of the barn. God, he missed her. If only he had kept his mouth shut and played his cards another way, she might be riding with him.

He almost smiled, something that had been in short supply since he'd lost her. Ellen on horseback wasn't going to happen. But that was okay. He didn't give a damn if she ever rode a horse or baited a hook.

He had made unreasonable demands on her. He realized that now. He'd known when he met her that she was a career woman who would never be comfortable wearing an apron.

Ass that he was, he'd tried to tie one on her. She'd been right about that. But only after he'd lost her did that fact hit him like a bullet in the head. Still, he was in love and wanted desperately to find the right words to make amends.

He couldn't. She'd gone back to Tyler. Having reached the barn, Porter groaned as he leapt off his horse. The thought of her dallying with her ex made him want to slam his hand through one of the walls, though that display of immaturity wouldn't accomplish anything except to injure his hand.

But he had to do something, dammit, to get her back.

When he walked into the kitchen, Bonnie was at the stove. For a minute a vision of Ellen standing there flashed through his mind. Wishful thinking.

Bonnie swung around, a troubled look descending over her features. "You miss her, don't you?"

Porter was taken aback. "Who?"

"You know who," Bonnie said with a testy smile.

"Yeah, I do."

"Do you love her?"

Porter didn't hesitate. "Yes, I do."

"So are you going to marry her?"

"If she'll have me," he finally said, a nerve working overtime in his jaw.

Suddenly Porter knew what he had to do. He was going the hell after her, and, if necessary, he would beg for another chance.

"I hope you'll be happy."

"Do you really mean that?"

His housekeeper averted her gaze. "Of course."

"If Ellen and I do work things out, would you continue to take care of Matt?"

For the first time he felt awkward around his housekeeper. But when Ellen had mentioned that Bonnie might think of him as more than an employer, it had rattled him. Discussing his personal life increased his apprehension.

"Probably not," Bonnie said gently. "My sister's been wanting me to move to North Carolina for a long time. Maybe now is that time."

"By saying now, you don't actually mean *now,* do you?" Porter didn't panic, but he came close to it.

"Of course not," she was saying. "Though I do know Lucy Evans would love to take my place."

Relief replaced the panic. Lucy would do just fine. She'd substituted for Bonnie when she'd taken vacations.

"Matt likes her, that's for sure," Porter said.

"Speaking of Matt, I hear him crying." Bonnie wiped her hands on a nearby towel. "I'll go get him."

"I'll kiss him goodbye, then I'm headed for Tyler."

Bonnie left the room, only to return seconds later, holding Matt, a frantic look on her face.

"What the hell...?"

"He's burning up with fever."

Porter cursed as he reached for his son. "Let's get him to the hospital."

Maybe she should just close the Nacogdoches store and remain in Tyler. She'd even thought of opening another Coffee, Anyone? across town from the other one.

Ellen had been there nearly two weeks, and she still hadn't been able to patch the hole in her heart left by Porter's exit from her life. She also missed the piney woods in general and, more specifically, her sister.

Surprising her even more, she missed Matthew. So what did all those unexpected emotions mean? She didn't know, maybe because she didn't want to explore them any further. That kind of exploration was too painful.

She'd been staying with Liz, something that couldn't continue indefinitely. If she remained in Tyler, she would have to find a place of her own. That was not a pleasant thought.

So what *was* pleasant? What would make her happy again? Having Porter's arms wrapped tightly around her and watching Matt grin his delightful grin were the answers that promptly came to mind.

Suddenly Ellen clutched the edge of the chest in Liz's guest bedroom, where she was getting dressed to go to the shop.

What should she do? Should she go back home? *Home.*

Funny that she should think of Nacogdoches as home and not Tyler. But home was where the heart was, and hers was definitely there, with Porter.

But she knew he'd meant what he said. And she could never live up to what he wanted. Or could she?

She would have to go back and find out.

Her thoughts were interrupted by the ringing of her cell phone. She snatched it off the bedside table.

"Sis, it's me."

"Hi, Meggy."

"I'm calling with bad news," Meg said bluntly.

Ellen held her breath, then released it. "Not Kyle again?"

"No, it's Matt. He's been taken to the hospital."

"Oh, my God. Do they know what's wrong with him?"

"Not yet, but I thought you'd want to know."

"Of course I want to know. Should I come home?"

"Are you asking my advice?" Meg's tone was sharp.

"Yes."

"Okay, here goes. You're damn right you should. Porter's crazy about you, and you're crazy about him. And you're both crazy if you throw that love away. So there, you got what you asked for."

"That I did."

"So what are you going to do?"

When Ellen arrived at the hospital a couple of hours later, she felt as if every nerve in her body was visible on the outside of her skin, and her mouth was so dry that she couldn't get enough saliva to swallow.

Not only was she concerned about the baby, but she was concerned about facing Porter. Meg could be wrong; she could have misread Porter. He might not be happy to see her at all.

Ellen didn't care. Happiness was a gamble. *Life* was a gamble. She'd made up her mind to throw the dice. If she won, then she would be ecstatic. If she lost, then she would pick up the pieces and glue them back together, just as she'd done before.

However, this time it wouldn't be so easy. What she had felt for Samuel in no way resembled her feelings for Porter. She hadn't known what love was until now.

She saw him right away.

He was striding down the corridor. When he saw her, his eyes narrowed, and he pulled up sharp.

She did the same. For what seemed an interminable length of time, they stared at each other. Ellen didn't bother to hide what was in her heart. She hoped all the love she felt for this man was written in every tiny line on her face.

Apparently it was, for an expression of pure joy overrode the grimness that was mirrored on his. Porter smiled and strode toward her. They met halfway, but he didn't touch her, not physically, anyway. However, his eyes touched her with heat-filled love.

"How's...how's Matt?"

"Fine now," he said in a low, strained voice. "It's just an infection."

"Thank God."

Silence.

"So is Matt why you came back?

"No. I had made up my mind before Meg called."

"Me, too."

Her eyes widened. "You mean you were coming to Tyler?"

"I was on my way out the door when I found out Matt was burning up with fever."

"Where...where do we go from here?" Her voice was barely audible.

He didn't answer. Instead he grabbed her hand and pushed her inside a door marked private.

"Porter!" she gasped when he slammed the door to the empty, semidark room and pushed her against the wall, grinding his mouth into hers. She gave him back as good as he gave.

When the kiss ended, Porter pressed his forehead against hers. "I've been dying for you."

"I love you."

"And I love you. Will you forgive me for being a hard-headed fool?"

"Only if you'll forgive me," Ellen said in a shaky voice.

"You're without sin here, my darling. I love you for the woman you are, not for the woman I want you to be."

"Oh, Porter, I—"

"Shush, let me finish. There's a difference, and you know it.

"I'm pretty pigheaded myself, so I'd say we're both at fault."

"Will you marry me?"

"Just say when."

"As soon as we can get a license."

Ellen's tongue snaked out and ran the length of his bottom lip. He groaned and pressed against her. "If you don't stop, I'm going to take you right here. I'm that hot and desperate."

"I'd let you, if I wasn't afraid we'd be interrupted."

He chuckled as he moved back. "Let's go get Matt, then we can go home."

"And make up for lost time."

He kissed her again.

"And while we're at it, maybe we can work on giving Matt a brother or sister."

Porter's eyes darkened, and his breath seemed to lock in his lungs for a second. "You mean that?"

"With all my heart."

"Then we'd better get a move on, my love. Time's a wastin'."

* * * * *

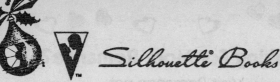

What do you want for Christmas?

A DADDY FOR CHRISTMAS

'Tis the season for wishes and dreams that come true. This November, follow three handsome but lonely Scrooges as they learn to believe in the magic of the season when they meet the *right* family, in *A Daddy for Christmas*.

MERRY CHRISTMAS, BABY
by Pamela Browning

THE NUTCRACKER PRINCE
by Rebecca Winters

THE BABY AND THE BODYGUARD
by Jule McBride

Available November 1998
wherever Harlequin and Silhouette books are sold.

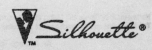

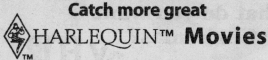

FOLLOW THAT BABY...

the fabulous cross-line series featuring the infamously wealthy Wentworth family...continues with:

THE SHERIFF AND THE IMPOSTOR BRIDE
by Elizabeth Bevarly
(Desire, 12/98)

When a Native American sheriff spies the runaway beauty in his small town, he soon realizes that his enchanting discovery is actually Sabrina Jensen's headstrong *identical* twin sister....

Available at your favorite retail outlet, only from

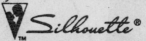